WELCOME TO ORSK!

Horrorstör is an original work of fiction, horror, and parody. The contents of this book are not sponsored by, affiliated with, or endorsed by any furniture retailer or manufacturer. The settings and characters described in this story do not exist in real life. All furniture and merchandise featured herein are products of the author's fevered imagination.

ORSK

Let Orsk Help You Be Yourself— the Orsk Way!

Choose...
YOURSELF!

Wind your way through our Showroom, explore design concepts, and sample combinations of furniture and fun.

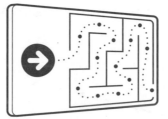

Pack...
YOURSELF!

Write down your choices and then find them in our easy-to-navigate Self-Service Warehouse. Orsk products are flat packed for easy transportation.

Pick...
YOURSELF!
Browse, shop, look, try. We'll show you how to be the best designer of your own life.

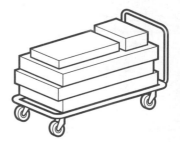

YOUR LIFE. YOUR STYLE. OUR FURNITURE.

Assemble...
YOURSELF!

Remember, Orsk voids all warranties if you ignore our clear and easy-to-follow assembly instructions.

Enjoy...
YOURSELF!

Orsk is a global leader in crafting quality furniture for every stage of every life. Let us help you be the best you that you can be!

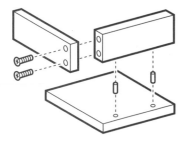

Orsk...
YOURSELF!

Store partners are here to help you craft your ideal kitchen, best bath, or ultimate shelving solution. If you ever have a question, just Orsk!

ORSK: THE BETTER HOME FOR THE EVERYONE!

ORSK
HOME DELIVERY ORDER FORM

BILL TO

Name

Street Address

City ___ State ___ ZIP ___

Phone ( ) -

E-mail

SHIP TO
(if different from bill to)

Name

Street Address

City ___ State ___ ZIP ___

Phone ( ) -

Would you like to be added to our mailing list? O Yes O No

Item #	Item Name	Qty.	Price	Total
			Item subtotal	
			Value of promo code discount	
			Deduct discount for order subtotal	
			Add sales tax to subtotal	
			Deduct subtotal of gift cards & Orsk Visa coupons	
			Express delivery—add $15 per address for <2 business days	
			Additional oversize delivery charge (if applicable; see product description)	
			2–5-day shipping	
			TOTAL	

PAYMENT METHOD

O Check/Money Order* O Orsk Visa**
O Mastercard O Amex O Gift Card O Promo Code

Card #

Name on Card

Expiration / /

Gift Card # ___ 4-digit PIN #

Promo Code #

2–5-Day Shipping Charges per U.S. Address

Order Subtotal/Shipping Charge	
Up to $25	$4.95
$25.01–$50	$6.95
$50.01–$100	$7.95
$100.01 and up	$9.95

***Text copyright © 2014 by Grady Hendrix. All rights reserved. No part of this book may be reproduced in any form without written permission from the publisher. Library of Congress Cataloging-in-Publication Number: 2013956140. ISBN: 978-1-59474-526-3. Printed in the United States of America. Typeset in Futura and Sentinel. Designed by Andie Reid. Cover diorama and photography by Christine Ferrara, call-small.com. Illustrations by Michael Rogalski. Production management by John J. McGurk. Quirk Books, 215 Church Street, Philadelphia, PA 19106. quirkbooks.com. 10 9 8

Want the Finest Flat-Packed Furniture and Household Accessories Delivered to Your Home? Just Orsk!

Our white glove home delivery service is available 7 days a week, 365 days a year. Let our home assembly technicians work around your schedule.

Our products are guaranteed to give 100% satisfaction in every way.*

PRICING: At Orsk, your satisfaction is important to us. We trust you will understand that despite our best efforts, we do make occasional errors. Orsk is not obligated to honor pricing errors that may occur from time to time.

COMMUNICATION FROM ORSK: We love to reach out to our customers! And you can choose how you hear from us—either via the Orsk catalog or via weekly e-mail updates. If you prefer to hear from us less frequently, please visit the My Account section of the Orsk website to update your preferences.

PRIVACY POLICY: Every now and then, we'll make our mailing lists available to quality companies whose products might be of interest to you. If you would prefer not to receive their mailings, please visit the My Account section of the Orsk website to update your preferences.

RETURNS: To return or exchange an item, follow the instructions on the packing slip enclosed with your order and send it back using the return label supplied. We cannot accept returns on personalized items or sale items purchased from our catalog or online. For complete details on our return policy for all items, visit www.orskusa.com.

HOME SHOPPING: Shopping at Orsk should be so easy you don't even need to think about it. Visit one of our convenient store locations or shop online or over the phone, whichever best suits you. Our website and our phone shopping system never sleep, they're open 24 hours a day, 7 days a week, so you can browse and buy Orsk lifestyle products in the day, at night, or anytime in between. We're ready when you are.

JUST ASK NOAH: "Never Offline, Always Helpful," Noah is our automated shopping concierge service. Check inventory availability over the phone, price-match online, arrange home delivery without leaving your chair, and learn helpful and fascinating product information from the comfort of your home. Noah is helpful, efficient, and useful. Like having a servant who is always anticipating how to deliver the comfort you deserve. And when you're finished with Noah he doesn't expect a tip, you can just hang up or log out. He'll be right there waiting for you when you come back.

INSTALLATION ADVISORS: Making sure your measurements are accurate is essential when purchasing cabinets, countertops, shelving, or even a sofa. Orsk can arrange for an Installation Advisor to visit your home for a low-cost and affordable measurement consultation. Spending a few cents now to avoid surprises later has never made more sense.

EXIST!: Orsk's new, free digital lifestyle and design magazine, *Exist!*, brings great designer tips, staging solutions, behind-the-scenes information, and dynamic content from across the Orsk family right to your desktop. You don't have to leave your home to experience the excitement of Orsk, because now it's coming into your home!

OUR CROWD: Get special member pricing and bonus perks when you join Our Crowd—the best crowd, the Orsk crowd! Just scan your Orsk Our Crowd Card at special member stations throughout our stores to enjoy discounts on select furniture and meals, free rolls, free spring water, and other exciting opportunities. Membership lasts a lifetime and includes your entire family, so bring them into the fold and let them experience the satisfaction and security that come from being a part of Our Crowd.

*Up to 90 days.

RSTÖR

A Novel by Grady Hendrix

Designed by
ANDIE REID

Illustrated by
MICHAEL ROGALSKI

Cover photography by
CHRISTINE FERRARA

ORSK
MILWAUKEE

QUIRK BOOKS
PHILADELPHIA

BROOKA

01

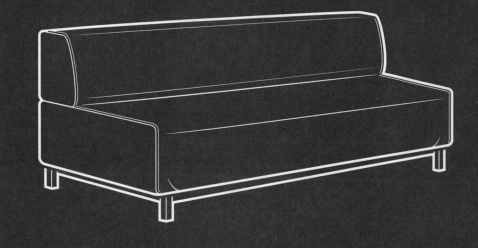

A sofa that's everything you ever dreamed a sofa could be. With memory-foam cushions and a high back that delivers the support your neck deserves, **BROOKA** is the relaxing beginning to the end of your day.

AVAILABLE IN FOREST GREEN, AUBERGINE, CARDINAL, AND NIGHT
W 87¾ X D 32¼ X H 34¼
ITEM NUMBER 5124696669

It was dawn, and the zombies were stumbling through the parking lot, streaming toward the massive beige box at the far end. Later they'd be resurrected by megadoses of Starbucks, but for now they were the barely living dead. Their causes of death differed: hangovers, nightmares, strung out from epic online gaming sessions, circadian rhythms broken by late-night TV, children who couldn't stop crying, neighbors partying till 4 a.m., broken hearts, unpaid bills, roads not taken, sick dogs, deployed daughters, ailing parents, midnight ice cream binges.

But every morning, five days a week (seven during the holidays), they dragged themselves here, to the one thing in their lives that never changed, the one thing they could count on come rain, or shine, or dead pets, or divorce: work.

Orsk was the all-American furniture superstore in Scandinavian drag, offering well-designed lifestyles at below-Ikea prices, and its forward-thinking slogan promised "a better life for the everyone." Especially for Orsk shareholders, who trekked to company headquarters in Milwaukee, Wisconsin, every year to hear how their chain of Ikea knockoff stores was earning big returns. Orsk promised customers "the everything they needed" in the every phase of their lives, from Balsak cradles to Gutevol rocking chairs. The only thing it didn't offer was coffins. Yet.

Orsk was an enormous heart pumping 318 partners—228 full-time, 90 part-time—through its ventricles in a ceaseless circular flow. Every morning, floor partners poured in to swipe their IDs, power up their computers, and help customers size the perfect Knäbble cabinets, find the most comfortable Müskk beds, and source exactly the right Lågniå water glasses. Every afternoon, replenishment partners flowed in and restocked the Self-Service Warehouse, pulled the picks, refilled the impulse bins, and hauled pallets onto the Market Floor. It was a perfect system, precision-engineered to offer optimal retail functionality in all 112 Orsk locations across North America and in its thirty-eight locations around the world.

But on the first Thursday of June at 7:30 a.m., at Orsk Location #00108 in Cuyahoga County, Ohio, this well-calibrated system came grinding to a halt.

The trouble started when the card reader next to the employee entrance gave up the ghost. Store partners arrived and piled up against the door in a confused chaotic crowd, helplessly waving their IDs over the scanner until Basil, the deputy store manager, appeared and directed them all to go around the side of the building to the customer entrance.

Customers entered Orsk through a towering two-story glass atrium and ascended an escalator to the second floor, where they began a walk of the labyrinthine Showroom floor designed to expose them to the Orsk lifestyle in the optimal manner, as determined by an army of interior designers, architects, and retail consultants. Only here was yet another problem: the escalator was running down instead of up. Floor partners shoved their way into the atrium and came to a baffled halt, unsure what to do next. IT partners jammed up behind them, followed by a swarm of post-sales partners, HR partners, and cart partners. Soon they were all packed in butt to gut and spilling out the double doors.

Amy spotted the human traffic jam from across the parking lot as she power-walked toward the crowd, a soggy cup of coffee leaking in one hand.

"Not now," she thought. "Not today."

She'd bought the coffee cup at the Speedway three weeks ago because it promised unlimited free refills and Amy needed to stretch her $1.49 as far as it would go. This was as far as it went. As she stared in dismay at the mass of partners, the bottom of her cup finally gave up and let go, dumping coffee all over her sneakers. Amy didn't even notice. She knew that a crowd meant a problem, and a problem meant a manager, and this early in the day a manager meant Basil. She could not let Basil see her. Today she had to be Basil Invisible.

Matt lurked on the edge of the semicircle, dressed in his usual black hoodie. He was glumly eating an Egg McMuffin and squinting painfully in the morning sun.

"What happened?" Amy asked.

"They can't open the prison, so we can't do our time," he said, picking crumbs from his enormous hipster beard.

"What about the employee entrance?"

"Busted."

"So how do we clock in?"

"Don't be in such a hurry," Matt said, trying to suck a strand of cheese off the mass of hair surrounding his mouth. "There's nothing waiting inside but retail slavery, endless exploitation, and personal subjugation to the whims of our corporate overlords."

If Amy squinted, she could dimly see Basil's tall, gawky silhouette through the front windows, trying to direct the human traffic jam by waving his spaghetti-noodle arms in the air. Getting even this close to him sent a cold bolt of fear through her stomach, but his back was turned. Maybe she had a chance.

"Good thoughts, Matt," she said.

Seizing her moment, Amy ninjaed her way through the crowd, ducking behind backs, stepping on toes, and slipping into open spaces. She entered the atrium and was immediately enveloped in the soothing embrace of Orsk—where it was always the perfect temperature, where the rooms were always perfectly lit, where the piped-in music was always the perfect volume, where it was always perfectly calm. But this morning the air had an edge to it, the faint scent of something rancid.

"I didn't think this escalator could run in reverse," Basil was saying to an operations partner who was pounding on the emergency stop button to no effect. "Is this even mechanically possible?"

Amy didn't stick around to find out. Her sole objective for the day—and for the next several days—was to avoid Basil at all costs. As long as he didn't see her, she reasoned, he couldn't fire her.

The Cuyahoga store had been operational for just eleven months, but it was already an open secret that it was falling short of corporate sales expectations. The failure wasn't due to a lack of customers. On weekends especially, the Showroom and Market Floor were packed with families, couples, retirees, people with nowhere else to go, college kids and their roommates, new families with their new babies, grim-faced couples buying their first sofas . . . a legion of potential customers, clutching maps, bags stuffed with lists of model numbers written on sticky notes, with torn-out pages from the Orsk catalog, credit cards burning holes in their pockets, all of them ready to spend.

Yet for some inexplicable reason, sales weren't hitting projections.

Amy had transferred to Cuyahoga from the Youngstown store fifty miles away. Initially she was okay with the move; she lived halfway between the two locations, and her commute hadn't changed. But after eleven months in Cuyahoga, she'd had enough. She filed a transfer request to get back to Youngstown, and now the computers at Orsk Regional were chewing over the paperwork. Help was on the way, if only she could last a few more days.

The problem was Basil, the newly appointed deputy store manager. A tall black guy with perfect posture and dry-cleaned work shirts, he'd been targeting Amy ever since his promotion. He was always coming into her shop to second-guess her decisions and offer advice she didn't want. She knew he was building an HR case against her, accumulating a long list of missteps and failures. When the staff cuts came—and everyone knew cuts were coming; you could sense a weird sort of tension in the air—Amy knew she would be at the top of Basil's list.

So she was on her best behavior while her transfer request made its way through the system. She arrived on time every day. She smiled at customers and didn't blink at last-minute schedule changes. She made sure her uniform (beige polo shirt, blue jeans, Chuck Taylor sneakers) was impeccable. She fought her natural tendency to talk back. And, most important, she steered clear of Basil, determined to stay off his radar.

With a high-pitched mechanical scream and the shredding of gears, the escalator came to a halt, then reversed direction. Basil tried to pat the operations partner on the back, while the operations partner tried to high-five Basil. The result was awkward.

"Way to live the ethos, man!" Basil cheered, clapping a few times.

Then the crowd of floor partners funneled onto the slotted steps, ascending to the second-floor Showroom.

Rather than follow everyone and walk right past Basil, Amy decided to go the long way. Defying the intentions of an entire think tank of retail psychologists, she walked backward through Orsk, starting at the rear (the checkout registers) and moving clockwise through its entire digestive tract toward its mouth (the Showroom entrance at the top of the escalator). Orsk was designed to move customers counterclockwise, keeping them in a state of retail hypnosis.

Going the opposite way felt like walking through a carnival spookhouse with all the lights turned on: the effect was ruined.

She ran past the registers and down the massive central aisle of the Self-Service Warehouse, with its soaring fifty-foot ceilings and towers of shelves. Flat-packed furniture rose up on tiers of industrial shelving, disappearing into the misty distance down endless gray rows. A bleak, prefabricated city built of cardboard and fourteen-gauge steel, the warehouse loomed over her for forty-one belittling aisles before she reached the sudden drop in ceiling height that marked the border crossing onto the Market Floor.

She rushed through the perfumed air of Home Decorations and its crates of scented candles, sped past the bland-tastic art of Wall Decorations, and pushed through the swinging-door shortcut that teleported her from the bulb-warmed air of the Lighting Gallery into Tableware, where she reached the staircase leading up to the Showroom.

Taking the steps two at a time, she surfaced next to the café on the Showroom floor. The Showroom was the centerpiece of the Orsk experience—an ocean of furniture awash with room displays staged to look like real homes decorated with Orsk furniture (all available for purchase in the Self-Service Warehouse downstairs). Amy zipped through Children's, heading for a shortcut between departments, when she noticed someone staring at her and skidded to a halt.

A man was standing in the distance, up near the Magog bunk beds, and even from far away Amy knew he wasn't a store partner. Orsk employees came in four different colors: floor partners in beige shirts, replenishment partners in orange shirts, operations partners in brown shirts, and trainees in red shirts. The man staring at Amy was dressed in dark blue. He didn't belong. He might have been a customer who sneaked in early.

But before she could investigate, the man turned and darted into Wardrobes. Amy just shrugged—whoever he was, he wasn't her problem.

Staying away from Basil until her transfer came through—*that* was her problem.

She took the shortcut into Storage Solutions, picked her way through several rows of Tawse and Ficcaro storage combinations, and finally emerged in the lowlands of Home Office, a shop populated with nothing but desks. Basil stood waiting next to the information post that Amy called home, with six trainees in red shirts clustered behind him.

"Good morning, Amy," he said. "I need you to take these trainees on the main aisle walk."

"I'd love to," Amy said, smiling so hard her face hurt. "But yesterday Pat asked me to floor-check inventory."

"I need you to take these trainees on the main aisle walk," Basil repeated. "Someone else can do the floor check."

Amy was about to protest further—something about Basil compelled her to argue with every word that came out of his mouth—when her cell phone unleashed a shrill Woody Woodpecker laugh, informing her that she'd received a text message. Basil watched in disbelief as she fumbled the phone out of her pocket.

"Of course," Basil announced to the trainees, "Amy

knows that partners are *never* permitted to bring their phones onto the Showroom floor."

"It's another help message," she explained, showing him the phone's screen.

A few weeks earlier, several floor partners had started receiving one-word texts reading *help* from the same private number. Proliferating like rabbits, the texts came pouring in at all hours, and they were freaking people out. Corporate claimed that IT was powerless to address the issue since it was technically not Orsk related. They advised partners to block the offending number or consult with their service providers. Amy had tried both suggestions, but the occasional *help* still slipped through.

"All partners must leave their phones in their lockers," Basil said, letting the full force of his disapproval fall on Amy like a rock. "Where Amy should have left hers before she clocked in."

That's when Amy realized she *hadn't* clocked in—she was essentially working for free until she could sneak back to the time clock and swipe her ID. She didn't dare mention this now, not with Basil already riding her case. Amy would honor the first commandment of keeping her job: Do not look like an idiot in front of anyone who can fire you.

"All right, everybody," she said, forcing a smile for Basil and controlling her panic. "My name is Amy and this is the Showroom floor. This is where every new customer begins their relationship with Orsk, so it's where we'll start, too. The store is 220,000 square feet, and our customers navigate the floor plan using the Bright and Shining Path." She pointed to a series of big friendly white arrows on the floor. "It's designed to take a customer from entrance to checkout in the optimal manner. There are shortcuts throughout the store, and I'll show you those when we get to them."

Amy had given this speech so many times, she was barely paying attention. Instead she was thinking about Basil and all the reasons she disliked him. It wasn't because he was three years younger and five promotions ahead of her. And it wasn't that he was skinny and geeky, all shoulder blades and elbows, a taller Urkel from *Family Matters*. And it wasn't the endless stream of phony inspirational corporate-speak that flowed out of him all day long. No—Amy's problem with Basil was that he acted like he felt sorry for her, like she was his charity case, like she required extra attention, and that made her want to punch him in the face.

"The typical customer spends three and a half hours on their first trip to Orsk, and most of that time is spent up here, in the Showroom. Our focus here is aspiration, not acquisition. We want to teach customers how elegant and efficient their lives can be if they're fully furnished with Orsk. The Bright and Shining Path encourages them to take their time and exposes them to a range of furniture possibilities. This is where we show them that although they came here for a Genofakte nesting table, it would look so much better next to a Reniflur floor lamp."

Basil had wandered off, apparently satisfied that she wouldn't screw up the tour. Amy walked backward on the path, and the trainees followed like a string of red-shirted ducklings.

"There are two kinds of shopper at Orsk," she continued. "Those who buy nothing, and those who buy everything. But the serious shopping doesn't happen until they get downstairs to the Market Floor, where they'll encounter what we call 'open-wallet' areas. These are designed to put customers under maximum retail stress. The goal is to get them to open their wallets and buy something, even a light bulb, because once we crack their wallets, they will spend, on average, $97 per visit."

They arrived in Living Rooms and Sofas, where Matt was wrestling a Brooka onto a flat cart with another partner. With Basil a safe distance away, Amy relaxed her tone, ditched her smile, and reverted to her usual sarcastic self.

"On our left we see a floor partner in his natural habitat," she announced. "To work in Living Rooms and Sofas, you have to be capable of lifting at least fifty pounds, which means only the partners with the hottest bodies work this BA. Does anyone know what BA stands for?"

"Business area?" a trainee with braces ventured.

"And what do we do in a BA?" Amy asked.

Silence. No one ever answered this question correctly, even though it was right on the cover of the employee manual.

"We distribute joy!" Amy answered. "We share the joy of Orsk!"

Two steps closer to Matt and the stink hit Amy full in the face: the smell of sun-baked Porta-Potty, hot Dumpster juice, and rotten seafood. It hit the trainees next, and they pulled their red shirts up over their noses. The Brooka's upholstery (Blarg, from the Classical line) was soiled with dark smears.

"I am glad we're seeing this," Amy told them. "One

of the many benefits of working at Orsk is the opportunity to interact with customers from all different walks of life. Including the sorts of people who change dirty diapers on expensive sofas."

"Actually," Matt said, "it was like this when we opened."

"Which means the closing partners left it for the opening partners to handle," she said. "Trainees, it is a dog-eat-dog world at Orsk."

Matt shook his head again. "I closed last night. When I left, this sofa was fine. No one knows how it happened."

"Exactly," Amy said. "Which is why every info post is equipped with Orsk-approved, nontoxic, hypoallergenic air freshener. Because when some lady drops her mutant baby's drippy diaper behind a sofa, you don't want your shop to smell like her beautiful overachiever's butt for the rest of your shift."

"Does that happen a lot?" one of the trainees asked.

"It never ends," Matt said. "People don't come here just to shop. Some of them think this is their living room, only with maid service. And you're the maid. They act like pigs, and you have to pick up after them. Dirty diapers are just the start. Last week I had a customer chewing tobacco and spitting into a Coke can, but he kept missing and covering the floor with brown oysters."

"And on that happy note," Amy said, "let us proceed to Storage Solutions, one of the least pleasant shops in Orsk because no one ever brings their exact measurements."

For the next two hours and ten minutes, Amy marched the trainees around the Showroom, from

Kitchens and Dining Rooms to Bedrooms, Bathrooms, Wardrobes, and Children's. She brought the tour to a close at the café around noon, pausing beside a wall of ten black-framed photographs of the store's senior management, all of them giving their best team player smiles.

"We end our journey at a gallery of accomplishment that you can only dream of joining," she said. "These men and women are the big brains behind Orsk. If you want to keep your job, I suggest you memorize their faces, learn their names, and avoid them like the plague."

As the trainees studied the wall—some were taking Amy seriously and trying to memorize the faces—Trinity appeared behind Amy.

"Do you believe in ghosts?" she asked.

Amy stepped back, startled. "Jesus!"

"I guess he counts as a ghost," Trinity said. "But I meant more of the *Paranormal Activity* type. I think there are two kinds of people in the world: people who believe in ghosts and people who don't. So which are you?"

Trinity was one of those happy, super-popular, high-energy girls who reminded Amy of the creatures from *Gremlins*: she was fun for about half an hour, then you wanted to stuff her in a blender. Supposedly her parents were super-Christian Koreans, which helped explain her rainbow-colored pigtails, her pierced tongue, the tramp-stamp on her lower back, and a full spectrum of multicolored fingernails. Despite the glam-punk look, Amy knew the nails cost $125, the hair was professionally dyed, the piercing cost a fortune, and the tattoo wasn't cheap, either.

Scratch a rebel, Amy thought, and you'll always find a father's credit card.

"Trainees, this is your lucky day," Amy said, turning to the huddle of red shirts. "Trinity works in Staging and Design, which is just a stepping-stone away from working on the catalog in the Orsk USA corporate office."

A handful of trainees perked up. The employees in Corporate had the best benefits and the best salaries. More important, they never had to deal with customers trying to game them for discounts by pointing out that Target sells a similar item, only cheaper, so couldn't they cut another twenty percent off the price?

The trainees began quizzing Trinity. How did she know when a room was successfully staged? How long did it take her to learn the Ninety-Nine Orsk Home Staging Solutions? Was it true that desks with fake computers sold six times better than desks without fake computers?

"HR will be here in a minute," Amy told the trainees. "They'll help you continue on your exciting journey with Orsk."

No one was listening to her anymore. All eyes were on Trinity.

"These are great questions!" she cheered. "But I'm only taking questions from true believers. How many of you have seen a ghost? Quick show of hands."

Amy left Trinity to baffle the trainees and walked back to Home Office to start her floor check. Ever since the Cuyahoga store opened eleven months ago, the computers were constantly burping up inventory mismatches. As a result, all day, every day, partners had to troop out onto the floor and hand count the inventory, over and over and over again. It was the kind of repetitive labor that killed your soul.

The latest victims of the inventory crisis were the Tossur treadmill desks, the first in Orsk's new line of exercise furniture. Amy thought they were insane. For her, the world was divided into two kinds of jobs: those where you had to stand up, and those where you could sit down. If you were standing up, you were paid hourly. If you were sitting down, you were salaried. Currently Amy's job was standing (bad), but she knew that one day, if she was lucky, she would have a job that was sitting (good). Tossurs took that universal standing/sitting truth and perverted it. Was a treadmill desk sitting or standing? Just thinking about it made her head hurt.

She was standing at her info post, pulling the inventory checklist, when Trinity suddenly reappeared.

"Gah!" Amy yelped.

"I forgot to tell you. Basil wants to see you in the motivation room. Closed-door coaching. And you know what that means."

Amy's face went numb with panic. "Did he say anything else? Did he tell you why?"

"Isn't it obvious?" Trinity said, grinning. "You are so fired."

DRITTSËKK 02

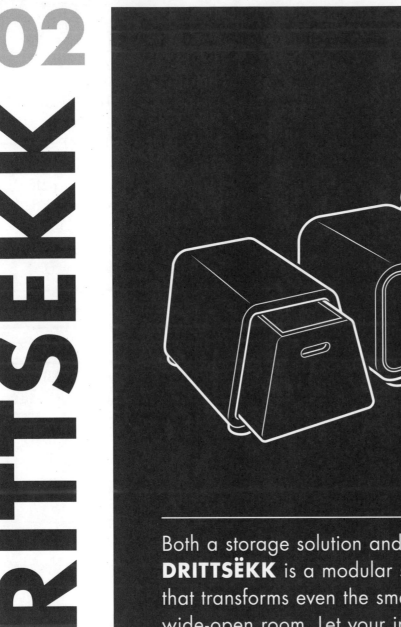

Both a storage solution and a place to rest, **DRITTSËKK** is a modular seating arrangement that transforms even the smallest space into a wide-open room. Let your imagination—and your friendships—roam.

AVAILABLE IN LIME, LEMON, FLAMINGO, SNOW, AND NIGHT
W 42¾ X D 32¼ X H 34¼
ITEM NUMBER 5498766643

Amy crossed the café and passed through the doors leading to the back of house. At the end of a long hallway lined with HR offices, IT offices, and sales offices, she slid open the door to the motivation room. Sitting alone on a Drittsëkk cube was a middle-aged woman who looked like a country-western singer, all big blond hair and too much mascara, nervously patting a tube of Blistex against her lips.

"Ruth Anne?" Amy asked in disbelief. "You, too?"

"Well," Ruth Anne said, trying to keep her voice under control and twisting the cap back on her lip balm. "I'm not jumping to any conclusions."

Amy closed the door and lowered herself onto another Drittsëkk sitting cube. Ruth Anne was as committed and responsible as Amy was lazy and untrustworthy. If Basil wanted to meet with both of them, the staff cuts had to be much worse than Amy imagined.

Her brain began chasing itself in circles. If Ruth

Anne was going, then she was definitely going. And if she was going, then everything was over. She'd lose her apartment. She'd have to move back into her mom's trailer. Working retail wasn't so bad if you got benefits and $12 an hour. But if she lost this job, she'd have no other option but mall retail, and all those jobs were minimum wage, and in Ohio that meant $7.95 an hour. She couldn't live on $7.95 an hour; she was behind on rent as it was. And if Ruth Anne was going, she was definitely going.

Around and around her brain went.

"Did they say anything to you?" Amy asked.

"No," Ruth Anne said. "But if we're both here, I'm sure Basil has a very good reason."

"We're the first ones to go," Amy said. "He's firing us."

"Let's make sure it's really raining before we worry about floods," Ruth Anne said. "This could turn out to be something nice."

That was Ruth Anne all over. She remembered birthdays, she remembered hiring-day anniversaries, she remembered children's names, she remembered what spouses did for a living, and she talked to older partners exactly the same as to younger ones. She never patronized, she never condescended, and she never said a mean word about anybody.

She'd worked at the Youngstown store for thirteen years before transferring to Cuyahoga "just to try something new." At forty-seven years old, she'd never married, didn't have kids, and Amy had never heard of a serious boyfriend. She treated Orsk like her family and home, and every day she tried to make it a better place. As a cashier in checkout, she considered it her personal mission to send customers out the door with smiles on their faces. She lived to make other people happy.

"I appreciate that you're looking on the bright side," Amy said. "But if you're here with me, it can't be good news."

"Don't you worry," Ruth Anne said, pressing her lips together. "We'll just sit right here and whatever comes, we'll get through it together."

Then she leaned over and gave Amy a hug. Amy tried to say something, but her tear ducts felt swollen and her throat was a clenched fist. She knew that if she opened her mouth to say anything, some great big honking sob would claw its way out. She promised herself that she was not going to cry. They could take her job, but they would not take her dignity. Amy pulled back from Ruth Anne, gritted her teeth, and stared down at the carpet.

How had it come to this? For the first eighteen years of her life, she'd had one goal: get out of her mom's trailer. When the guidance counselor had laughed at her plans to go to college, she'd cobbled together enough grants to get into Cleveland State for commercial design. But then her mom remarried, and her new husband's income had pushed Amy into another need bracket. Without financial aid, she had to file papers as a noncontinuing student. Now she was late with her rent again, and her three roommates had made it clear that she had twenty-four hours to deliver the $600 she owed or they would throw her out.

The more Amy struggled, the faster she sank. Every month she shuffled around less and less money to cover the same number of bills. The hamster wheel kept spinning and spinning and spinning. Sometimes she wanted to let go and find out exactly how far she'd fall if she just stopped fighting. She didn't expect life to be fair, but did it have to be so relentless?

Ruth Anne squeezed Amy's hand and offered her a clump of Kleenex. Amy waved it away.

"I'm fine," she said. "I'm not crying."

The two women sat next to each other, stiff and silent. Amy moved from shock to bargaining, to depression, and right on through to righteous indignation, finally arriving at acceptance. Then her cycle of grief started all over again and by the time Basil slid open the door, she was back to righteous indignation. Before Basil could speak, Amy took the floor. If she was going down, she'd go out in a blaze of glory.

"I know you've got it in for me and that's fine. But I cannot believe that you are firing the one decent, good person in this place."

"What?" Basil asked, caught off guard.

"Amy, don't—" Ruth Anne began.

"No," Amy said. "If I'm getting fired, I'll take it. But I want him to know that firing you is a huge mistake." She turned to Basil. "Firing Ruth Anne is like clubbing a baby seal. It makes you evil. *Everyone* likes Ruth Anne."

"Amy, listen to me," Basil said. "Your brand connection is weak, your presentation leaves a lot to be desired, your attitude is aggressive and confrontational and not at all consistent with Core Values—"

"Don't do it," Amy said. "Please."

"—but I'm not firing you," Basil finished.

"You're not?" Amy asked.

"You're firing *me*?" Ruth Anne squeaked.

"I'm not firing either of you," Basil said. "I've asked you here because I need your help. I have an extra job for tonight. A side project. And I need you to keep quiet about it."

Relief flooded Amy's veins like a drug. In that moment, she would have agreed to anything: climbing Mount Everest, hijacking a plane, running naked across Orsk's ten-acre parking lot while playing the trombone. She nodded like a happy idiot, right along with Ruth Anne. But even as she did, the part of her brain that wasn't flooded with endorphins whispered, *It's going to be something weird. It has to be something weird.*

"It's going to be a little weird," Basil confirmed.

"How weird?" Amy asked.

Basil lowered his voice to action-movie-briefing volume. "We've seen a lot of crimes against the store over the past six weeks. Opening shift is finding damaged merchandise every morning. Mirrors, dishes, picture frames, curtains yanked down from the walls. A whole mattress hacked to shreds. And this morning we had . . . an incident. With a Brooka."

"Incident?" Ruth Anne asked.

"It was smeared with a substance," Basil said.

"Poop," Amy clarified.

"A substance," Basil repeated.

"That smelled like poop."

"We're eleven percent over on breakages, and Pat had to notify Regional. He's also tasked me to lead an internal investigation."

Pat was general manager of the entire store and Basil's direct superior. He once delivered a baby on a

Müskk, and he paid out of his own pocket for a karaoke DJ at the Christmas party. No one wanted to disappoint Pat.

"Naturally," Basil continued, "I don't want to disappoint him."

"What about Loss Prevention?" Ruth Anne asked. "Don't they have cameras?"

"Hundreds," Basil said. "And I've reviewed the footage. But the lights are on a timer and at two o'clock every morning they power down to twilight mode. I've decided that's when the damage must be happening. Between 2 and 7:30 a.m., when the opening shift arrives."

"But that's impossible," Amy said. "No one's ever here after eleven."

"Apparently someone is," Basil said.

"I don't like the sound of this," Ruth Anne said, chewing her lip.

"I'm proposing that the three of us work an extra shift. Tonight, from ten to seven. We'll wait in the break room, and once an hour we'll do patrols of the store. The Showroom, the Market Floor, and the Self-Service Warehouse. If a vandal is sneaking in and trashing the place, we'll bust him and call the cops. Problem solved."

"I can't do tonight," Amy said. "I've got plans." This wasn't exactly true, but she didn't relish the idea of being awake for twenty-four hours.

"It has to be tonight," Basil said. "Regional already replied to Pat's e-mail. They're sending a Consultant Team first thing tomorrow morning. They'll want a full tour of the store. And they cannot arrive to find a Brooka smeared with . . . you know."

"Why us?" Amy asked.

"Because you're both loyal and reliable partners."

Amy rolled her eyes. "Seriously."

Basil hesitated. "All right, I'll be honest. I had Tommy and Gregg from Replenishment all lined up, but the Indians are playing the Sox, so they backed out. Then I asked David Potts and his brother Russell, but this morning they called in sick. So I tried Eduardo Pena, but he has to watch his grandchildren. Then I tried Tania from Café, but she's watching an eBay auction. Now I'm asking you, because I know you'll both say yes."

"Really?" Amy asked. "You're positive?"

"Ruth Anne will agree because she's discreet, she's responsible, and she cares about Orsk. You'll agree because you want to go back to Youngstown. I saw your transfer request on the computer this morning. I know you don't like this store, and I know you don't like me. But if you work this extra shift, I'll make sure your transfer goes through, and you won't ever have to see me again."

Amy's instinct was to fire back with a wisecrack, but she was startled to realize his proposal actually sounded pretty good. "You'll pay time and a half?"

"Even better: double overtime," Basil said. "In cash at the end of the shift. Just to show how much I appreciate your participation and your discretion."

Amy quickly did the math: eight hours at double overtime would net her two hundred dollars, enough to keep her roommates at bay until her next paycheck.

"Count me in," she said.

"Me, too," Ruth Anne said. "It'll be fun. Like a sleepover party."

Basil shook their hands, sealing the deal.

"Meet me at the employee entrance at ten o'clock," he explained. "I'll let you inside while Operations finishes cleaning. We'll wait in here until everything's quiet, then we'll do our first sweep. And not a word to anyone, understand? This is a covert operation."

The door to the break room burst open and Matt and Trinity tumbled inside. "There's people in here," Trinity exclaimed, feigning surprise.

"Hey, guys," Matt said. "What's up?"

Basil immediately tried to act like nothing was going on, which made it look like something was absolutely going on.

"We were just dialoguing," he said. He turned to Amy and Ruth Anne. "Thank you for your feedback. It's been duly noted and I'll pass it along."

"Feedback about what?" Matt asked.

"Is everything okay?" Trinity asked, searching Amy's eyes for clues. "There's a real weird energy in this room. Like someone's just had a difficult conversation."

"You better be on your break," Basil said as he headed out the door. "I've got to get back."

Trinity sat down across from Amy and Ruth Anne. "Seriously, what did he want? Are you guys fired? You can talk to me."

"Were you two creeping around the hall eavesdropping?" Amy asked.

"We're gathering information that is critical to staff morale," Trinity said.

"No one's fired," Ruth Anne said.

"Told you so," Matt said to Trinity. "I knew they'd never fire Ruth Anne."

Trinity stuck out her tongue, and she and Matt began to flirt-fight. Amy had heard that Trinity and Matt were hooking up, but she'd also heard the same rumor about Trinity and half the floor partners, male and female. She was the sort of revved-up party girl that guys found irresistible and Amy found irritating.

"I gotta go," she said, standing up.

Trinity put herself between Amy and the door. "If you weren't getting fired, what did Basil want? Do you have to do diversity training? Is he putting you on part-time? Is the store closing?"

"Sorry not to give you your daily allowance of store drama," Amy said. "But I've got more important things to do. Like floor checking Tossurs."

"Matt and I have used science to show that big changes are coming," Trinity said. "Things in this store are approaching a crisis point. Any information you have will help us complete the big picture."

"Seriously," Matt said. "Is the store closing?"

"Come on, Ruth Anne," Trinity said. "What happened? We need hard data."

"I think it's probably best if I don't say anything," Ruth Anne said.

"You're killing us," Trinity said. "You are literally killing us."

"Good," Amy said. "Maybe then you'll stop being so annoying."

And with that, Amy abandoned Ruth Anne to the two most irritating people in Orsk and walked back to her shop where she spent the next two hours comparing Tossur inventory numbers.

When her shift ended at four o'clock, Amy drove around for half an hour, then decided to get some sleep before the secret overnight shift began at ten. She couldn't risk going back to her apartment without the money she owed, and Basil had made it clear she wasn't getting paid until the overnight shift was finished. She was too embarrassed to nap in the Orsk parking lot with all of her coworkers walking by, so she drove a mile down Route 77, pulled into the parking lot of a Red Lobster, parked by the Dumpster, and leaned her seat all the way back.

It was hot, the interior of her car stank of oil, and her feet smelled like coffee. Amy closed her eyes, trying to still the buzzing in her head. At first she didn't think she'd be able to fall asleep, but the day had been long and her emotions were toast. After forty-five minutes of sitting and staring and thinking about what a wreck her life had become, after forty-five minutes of wondering how she was ever going to escape Orsk and get a sit-down job, after forty-five minutes of feeling sweat trickling down her ribs, she fell into a state of sticky semiconsciousness. And as her mind closed up shop and went dark, Amy wondered dully if she would be stuck on the hamster wheel forever, stuck in retail forever, stuck at Orsk forever.

But she didn't have to worry.

Tonight would be her final shift.

It's Not Just a Job.
It's the Rest of Your Life.

Interested in joining the Orsk family? Our entry-level partner positions offer competitive salaries with room for growth. Once you're here, you'll never want to leave!

AVAILABLE POSITIONS INCLUDE:

Staging & Design Partners

Develop range prestige, perform daily visual display maintenance, and proactively respond to upper-level directives regarding the commercial calendar for seasonal success.

Shopkeepers

Develop a deeper understanding of the Orsk core concepts and communicate this knowledge to visitors with maximum sales competence in your area of responsibility utilizing direct mouth-to-ear retail communication.

Cart Partners

Contribute to an environment where Orsk culture is a strong and living reality that embraces the diversity of Partners and Visitors. Must be able to lift 75 pounds.

 LET YOU BECOME WE—AT ORSK!

ARSLE

We're all morning people if we treat our bodies and minds with care and respect. Pause at your **ARSLE** to turn breakfast into a celebration of a brand new day. Sitting here, suddenly everything tastes just a little bit better.

AVAILABLE IN GOLDENROD, HONEYDEW, SALMON, AND PLUM
W 23¾ X D 30¼ X H 32¼
ITEM NUMBER 7666585634

During the day, Orsk was a building like any other, a sensible container built with modern materials to house furniture and people. But after eleven o'clock, when no one roamed its aisles, when its back offices went dark and the last customers were escorted out the front doors, when its entrances were dead-bolted, when its final floor partners went home, it became something else.

Amy, sitting on a toilet in the women's restroom on the second floor, was unaware of the subtle changes taking place around her. All she knew was that Basil was trying to kill her.

They were just one hour into the marathon overnight shift, and he would not stop bothering her. What did she like about her job? Which parts were most rewarding? Least rewarding? Amy had answered like an actual human being until she realized his questions were nothing more than the opening of a very boring lecture on the importance of human capital in

Orsk culture. He spoke at length on the value of team-work, about store pride, about the Four A's (Approach-able and Agreeable Attitude). He quoted Orsk founder Tom Larsen's autobiography from memory.

Ruth Anne was pretending to listen, but Amy could see that she was secretly doing Sudoku under the table—and if she could see it, Basil could see it, but he didn't seem to care. Why was he only target-ing Amy? She wanted to tell him she was doing just fine, that she didn't need his life advice, thankyou-verymuch. He already knew she was transferring back to Youngstown, so why couldn't he leave her alone? Torn between saying something or suffering in silence, Amy sought sanctuary in the bathroom.

If Basil cares so much about Orsk, he should come in here and clean, she thought. The walls of her stall were covered with graffiti. If it had been funny ("Pull here for MFA Degree" right below the toilet paper dis-penser) she would've stayed longer, but it was mostly weird random names and dates. After wiping and flushing, she walked to the sink, soaped her palms, fingers, and wrists, and then lathered them up again, trying to drag out the time before she had to return to the break room.

When she got back, Basil checked his watch. "That's your third trip to the restroom in an hour."

"And that's your business why?"

"Because you're here to do floor sweeps. Not hide in the bathroom all night."

Amy gritted her teeth. "I'll do your little floor sweeps. Just tell me when you're ready."

She marched back to her seat. The break room was furnished with Arsle tables and chairs; they were affordably priced and had a simple elegant design, but Amy couldn't last fifteen minutes in one without getting a backache. Ruth Anne sat quietly with three tubes of Blistex lined up on the table and the Sudoku book hidden on her knees.

Next to the door was a giant plastic bucket full of Magic Tools. The geniuses in Milwaukee designed their furniture to be incompatible with ordinary household tools; Orsk products could be assembled only with the proprietary Orsk Magic Tool. The small, L-shaped wrench was famously easy to lose, so the store gave them away by the bucketful and employees were required to carry one at all times. Amy had one in her pocket right now—and another dozen rolling around her junk drawer at home.

She glanced around the room. Over on the wall was a large banner that read: "The hard work makes Orsk a family, and the hard work is free." The completely fake, slightly stilted Euro-phrasing was part of Orsk's fake Ikea act, and Amy couldn't decide if it was slightly annoying or totally offensive. In her opinion, nothing was worse than a store that pretended to be something it was not.

There was nothing else in the break room to occupy Amy's eyes or mind. A flat-screen TV hanging in the corner displayed a soundless CNN broadcast. On it, a bunch of prisoners in orange overalls were being marched in a circle around a concrete exercise yard. Amy knew the feeling.

Basil dragged his chair over to Amy's table. "You know, I was really sorry when I saw your transfer request. I think you have a lot of potential. With a little hard work, I really think you could be Shop

Responsible."

"Thank you," she said, not taking her eyes off the television.

"I mean it, Amy. I used to be a floor partner like you. Then I took the test and became Shop Responsible, and soon I was a shopkeeper, then floor manager, then Pat moved me up to deputy store manager. If I can do it, you can, too."

"Right, and then I'll be on my way to management, which means I'll be responsible for everything that happens in this store, I'll be blamed every time something goes wrong, I'll have to go to more meetings, I'll have to work more hours, I'll have to deal with everyone's scheduling headaches, and I'll be making a whopping seventy-five cents more per hour. I'm not taking the test."

"You already did," Basil said. "Pat told me."

Ruth Anne perked up. "Really? That's terrific. Congratulations, Amy!"

Amy tried to keep herself under control.

"What's the matter?" Ruth Anne asked, genuinely concerned.

The silence grew.

"It's an easy test," Ruth Anne said, chattering on. "You just read the handbook for twenty minutes and fill in the bubbles . . ." Her voice trailed off.

"She didn't pass," Basil explained. "She was two points shy. I asked Pat to ask Regional if they would make an exception, but you know how they feel about business metrics. Numbers never lie, and all that."

Amy's face flushed. Everyone joked that the Shop Responsible test was so easy, "even a store manager could pass." Amy had been so confident that she hadn't even attempted to prepare for it. She just assumed she would sail right through.

"You can try again in six months," Basil said. "If you stick around, I'll help you study."

"I don't want your help," Amy said. "You started out in Wardrobes."

"What's that supposed to mean?" Basil asked.

"Wardrobes is the lamest shop on the floor," Amy said. "A packet of grape jelly could be Shop Responsible for Wardrobes. They're just big empty boxes with doors."

"That reveals a flawed understanding of Wardrobes," Basil said.

"Wardrobes is hard," Ruth Anne chimed in. "People get angry because they're so tough to put together."

"Okay," Amy said, taking a breath. "I'm sorry. Wardrobes is awesome. It's right up there with brain surgery. I shouldn't have said anything."

"If you don't want to be here, you don't have to stay," Basil said.

"I want to be here," Amy said, digging her nails into her palms. "But, no offense, I don't need any more advice, and please don't quote any more chapter titles from Tom Larsen's memoir. I know this is your religion, but for me it's just a job."

"That's your problem," Basil said. "For you it's 'just' a job."

"What's it supposed to be?"

"*Work.*"

"Same thing," Amy said.

"No," Basil said. "A job is what a guy in a gas station has. People at Orsk have work. It's a calling. A responsibility to something bigger than yourself.

Work gives you a goal. It lets you build something that lives on after you're gone. Work has a purpose beyond making money."

"I am begging you to stop," Amy said.

"There's nothing wrong with being serious," Ruth Anne said.

"She can't take anything seriously," Basil said. "That's her problem."

"I do my job," Amy said. "I punch the clock, I work my shop, I sell people their desks, I cash my check. That's what Orsk pays me to do: my job. I'm not planning on being in retail for the rest of my life."

"Really? What are you going to do?"

"I'm . . ." Amy suddenly realized that in fact she didn't have any plans. "I've got plans. They're none of your business."

"You have to see the big picture," Basil said.

"You know what I see? I see you dedicating your life to a store that's a knockoff of a *better* store with *better* furniture and *better* management. That's the big picture I see."

"Maybe we should start our first sweep," Ruth Anne said.

"I have serious responsibilities and I take them seriously," Basil said.

"What responsibilities?" Amy asked. "Seriously. This is retail. What is such a big deal?"

"Safety," Basil said. "I'm responsible for the safety of you and everybody else in this location. I take that very seriously."

"I can make it through my day without your protection," Amy said. "I'm not going to get lost and starve to death somewhere on the Showroom floor."

"I don't get your attitude," Basil said. "You want a promotion, but you don't study for the test. You don't want to work retail the rest of your life, but you dropped out of college. Do you really have some big plan, or are you just making it up as you go along?"

Amy stood up.

"Where are you going?" Basil asked.

She headed out the door. "To the bathroom."

"You just went!" he called after her.

Amy crashed through the door of the women's restroom. It was the only place Basil wouldn't follow her, yapping about a bunch of crap and trying to make her feel bad. Didn't he understand she was humiliated enough without him piling on? Eighty percent of applicants passed the Shop Responsible test. Eighty percent! Amy turned on the sink. The pipes made an obscene grunting sound that rattled the porcelain, and then they spat rusty water into the basin. Amy turned off the taps and shook her head. *This whole place is going to hell.*

She took deep breaths, trying to calm down. What was happening to her? She looked up at the reflection of her blotchy face. Her eyes drifted to the right-hand side of the mirror and her breath stopped. There was new graffiti.

Next to the mirror, she saw a fresh patch of writing that hadn't been there earlier. Or maybe it had?

Archie Wilson
BEEHIVE
3 years

YANCY RAWLS
Beehive
6 MONTHS

J. BUXTON
BEEHIVE
2 YR.

What in the world was the Beehive? A football team? A gang of Cleveland drug dealers? Some twenty entries were scratched into the paint, and all of them followed the same format: a name, the word "Beehive," and a time span. Closer to the door, she saw more graffiti with a few variations:

KIT BOERER
BEEHIVE
2 years
5 yr

Lows the Eyes
1 year
6 years

And the longest of the bunch:

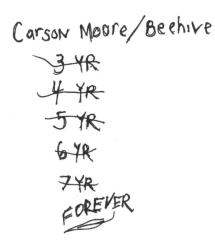

Carson Moore/Beehive
~~3 YR~~
~~4 YR~~
~~5 YR~~
~~6 YR~~
~~7 YR~~
FOREVER

Amy dried her hands on her jeans and left the restroom. In the hall, she could feel the empty spaces of Orsk all around her, 220,000 square feet isolating her in the middle of a maze. The service hallways, the back of house, the Warehouse, the Market Floor, the Showroom, the immense parking lot that separated them from the highway. Orsk was so big it needed a certain number of people on the premises to keep it under control. Three of them weren't enough. The store was stirring, restless, growing slowly. Emptied of people, Orsk felt dangerous.

SLAM!

Amy froze. What was that noise?

SLAM-CLICK-SLAM!

The corridor stretched out ahead of her, with doors to the management offices on either side. On the walls were posters about sustainability, green living for a green planet, Orsk's commitment to future generations, and there was a stairwell nearby leading down to the first floor. That's where the noise was coming from. Seconds passed and the loudest sound was Amy's breathing.

She took a deep breath and forced herself to be practical. She was at her job. She couldn't possibly be in any danger. No one had ever been murdered in a Best Buy or kidnapped in a Target. If there was a safer location than a big box retail outlet owned by a global corporation, she couldn't imagine it.

And yet she couldn't shake her unease. She descended the stairs to the first floor and stopped at the bottom.

Now the noise was much softer: *click, slam . . . click, slam . . . click, slam . . .*

Just past the time clock, Amy saw the door to the partners' entrance banging in the wind. Relieved, she smacked the exit bar and pushed it open, revealing the parking lot stained a chemical orange by sodium lights. She blinked, surprised to see that it was the middle of the night. Inside the store there were no windows, no skylights, no wall clocks, no way of telling the time or the temperature. Like a casino, Orsk existed in an eternal now. A warm, humid breeze flowed through the doorway. Apart from an unseen army of frogs croaking in the marsh, the night was completely silent.

Amy could see her little red Honda across the parking lot. She wished she could walk across the warm asphalt, slide behind the steering wheel, and drive . . . where? She couldn't go home without the money she owed her roommates. She couldn't leave without losing her job. She had nowhere to go.

Amy slammed the door of the partners' entrance harder than she intended, and a shower of paint flakes rained from the ceiling. The door wouldn't close, and she realized that something was jammed in the latch to keep it from striking home. Chewing gum, a giant pink wad of it. Amy contemplated digging it out, then decided that cleaning up gum was beyond her job description. If Basil wanted to be so responsible, *he* could tackle it.

He was frowning when she returned to the break area. "You can't keep hiding in the toilet stalls. We need to start our sweeps."

"The partners' entrance is broken," Amy said.

"Why were you downstairs?"

"I heard the door banging, so I decided to be responsible. Someone messed up the lock. You can't close it."

"A security breach," Basil said. "You see? This is exactly why we're here tonight!"

He raced off to investigate. Ruth Anne closed her Sudoku book. "You think someone really sneaked into the store?"

"I don't know what's going on," Amy said. "But there's new graffiti in the bathroom, and I'd swear it wasn't there twenty minutes ago."

"I'm starting to feel like I shouldn't have done this," Ruth Anne said, toying with the cap of her Blistex. "I wanted the extra hours, but I just figured I could do my puzzles. I didn't think we'd actually see anybody."

"Nothing bad is going to happen," Amy said, just before Woody Woodpecker's laugh filled the room. She checked her phone: *help.*

"I turn off my phone when I'm in the building," Ruth Anne said. "That way I never get them."

Basil burst into the room, sounding winded. "I got it closed but I can't lock it. We've definitely had a security breach," he announced. "We'd better start patrolling the floor right away."

He walked over to the dry-erase board, drew a rough map of the store, and started writing down their schedule. "I've divided the store so it's easier to search, and I've assigned everyone a zone. For this first pass, Ruth Anne will do the Showroom. Amy, you'll cover the Market Floor, and I'll tackle the Self-Service Warehouse."

"Wait, we're splitting up?" Ruth Anne asked.

"There's a lot of ground to cover," Basil explained.

"I don't think that's a good idea," Amy said. "And there's some graffiti in the women's bathroom you need to see."

"Graffiti is the least of my worries," Basil said.

"It's kinda weird—"

"I'd feel a lot safer if we all walked together," Ruth Anne said. "What am I supposed to do if I find someone? I mean, that's the idea, isn't it? You *want* me to find someone. But what happens when I do? And I'm all by myself?"

Basil suddenly looked like he had a very bad headache. Clearly he had put a lot of time and effort into drawing his diagram without thinking through the details. Splitting up might have been a viable option when a bunch of flat-pack-wrangling roughnecks like Tommy, Gregg, and the others were going to patrol the store, but what would Ruth Anne do if she encountered an intruder all alone? What would any of them do? Demonstrate an Agreeable and Approachable Attitude?

"If we travel together, we're too easy to evade," Basil said. "We need to split up. We'll have a bigger search footprint that way."

"Ruth Anne and I will go together," Amy said. "Think of the liability issues. We'll cover the Showroom, and you do the Market Floor and the Warehouse."

The mere mention of the word "liability" convinced Basil to accept the proposal. "Fine, but we need to get started right away," he said. "For all we know, someone's out there right now trashing store property."

It was nearly 11:30 p.m. when they emerged on the Showroom floor, next to the café with Children's to their left. Just ahead was the stairwell that led down to the Market Floor.

"Stay alert and keep your eyes peeled," Basil said in his best leader-of-men voice. "We'll meet back in the break area after this first patrol. If anything happens tonight, that's where we'll regroup, okay? And if you see anything suspicious, call me immediately. I've been trained for these situations. Remember: your safety is my responsibility."

"Right," Amy sighed.

They split up.

LIRIPIP 04

Clear the room and clear away your worries. No matter what size your home, the **LIRIPIP** wardrobe offers a place to store the things you need but don't want to look at every day.

AVAILABLE IN NATURAL BEECH, LIGHT MAPLE, AND GRAY OAK
W 19¾ X D 15¼ X H 72¼
ITEM NUMBER 4356663223

Amy cut through the café toward the top of the escalator.

"We'll follow the Bright and Shining Path," she said.

Then she realized there was no one walking beside her. She turned and saw Ruth Anne lingering on the other side of the café.

"I'm sorry," Ruth Anne called. "Do you want to check the café first? I'm not even really sure what we're looking for."

"Teenagers? Insomniacs? I don't know," Amy said. "Come on, we'll do the café last."

"Are you sure?"

"If you want to do the café first, we can do the café first."

"No, you're right," Ruth Anne said. "We'll do it your way."

She didn't move.

"Are you coming?" Amy asked.

"I'm sorry," Ruth Anne said, finally walking across the café to Amy. "This Showroom feels spooky. It's so different from the Youngstown store."

"They're exactly the same," Amy said.

"Why would anyone sneak into a store?" Ruth Anne said. "You've never actually seen that happen, have you?"

"Customers do all kinds of crazy things," Amy said. "I remember this giant fat dude who came in one day near closing, took off his shoes, folded up his pants, and crawled into a Müskk and fell asleep. No one even noticed him for an hour. And Pat told me that once he found some woman and her kid hiding in a Lingam after hours. He was walking through Bedrooms and the door of the wardrobe opened and the two of them came creeping out. He almost died."

They reached the top of the escalator. Before Amy turned onto the Bright and Shining Path, she paused at the line of framed photos showcasing store management.

"You know," she said, "I like Basil a lot better when his mouth isn't moving."

Ruth Anne looked like she wanted to say something sharp. Then she stopped herself.

"He's a nice young man."

"He's a tool bag," Amy said.

"Not everyone you disagree with is a bad person," Ruth Anne said.

"Basil is."

"He has a lot of responsibilities," Ruth Anne said.

"Like what?" Amy asked. "Making sure that every unit goes out minus one screw? Making the schedule suck for as many partners as possible?"

"He's raising his little sister," Ruth Anne said. "She's nine years old, and Basil's practically her daddy. He pays for everything, from her socks to her school fees."

Amy shuffled through her playlist of possible comebacks and came up short.

"Okay, I didn't know that," she said. "But he still sounds like a company training video. 'Orsk this, Orsk that, worship Orsk, hail Orsk.'"

"Orsk has been real good to him," Ruth Anne said. "He's from East Cleveland. Have you seen what that place looks like?"

Only on the ten o'clock news, Amy thought.

"When he started here, he was on the verge of giving up. Orsk gave him a job and turned his life around. Some people get church, some people get A.A., others get gangs. Basil got Orsk."

Conversations like this were frustrating because what could Amy say? Either she could agree that St. Basil needed a church named after him, or she could reply with some sarcastic remark that would make her seem petty. She'd had a lousy life, too, growing up in a crappy trailer with a mom whose idea of family time was playing Hide the Vodka. But if she brought that up now it would look like she was trying to compete with Basil, and there was no way she could win a Who's Got It Worse? contest. Not with someone who grew up black in East Cleveland.

"Let's just do our stupid patrol," Amy said.

Then she turned away from the escalator and followed the arrows past a giant stack of Orsk catalogs, at the entrance of Living Rooms and Sofas.

"You know," Ruth Anne said, "I worked in the

Youngstown store for thirteen years without ever having a problem in the Showroom. But the first day I started here, I got real lost. Not the funny kind of lost, either. This was the scary kind."

Amy wasn't listening. She was still smarting over her argument with Basil about the stupid Shop Responsible test. It wasn't failing that bothered her. It was everyone *knowing* that she failed.

Ruth Anne kept chattering away. "I was going to visit Diane in Kitchens. You know Diane Darnowsky? She wears all those Santa Claus buttons around Christmastime? Well, I was going out to see her, but I got so turned around, it took me half an hour. My whole lunch break. Scared the dickens out of me. I was panicking, thinking the store was actually moving around behind my back. By the time I reached Diane I just wanted to sit down and cry myself silly. I never went back out on the floor again."

"Are you serious?" Amy asked. "You've been here eleven months and you've never gone out on the Showroom floor?"

"You change when you get older," Ruth Anne said. "You'll see."

"It is weird in here with no people," Amy admitted. Ruth Anne's nerves were probably rubbing off on her. She started humming the theme from *The Twilight Zone*: "Doo-dee-doo-doo, doo-dee-doo-doo."

"Stop, please," Ruth Anne said. "It's bad enough without you doing that."

Amy stopped at a dun-colored information post. A map of the Showroom was painted on the side, with a giant YOU ARE HERE marker right in the middle of Living Rooms and Sofas. "It's just a big loop like every other Orsk. Just like Youngstown," she said, tracing a circle through the map. "I gave a tour to a bunch of trainees this morning. They picked it up right away."

Ruth Anne looked at the map the way a cat watches TV. Amy could tell that she had no clue what she was seeing.

"See where it says YOU ARE HERE?" Amy asked.

"Mm-hm," Ruth Anne said, unconvincingly.

"That's where we are. There's a map in every department so you can find your way. Like a trail of bread crumbs. As long as you're paying attention, you can't get lost."

Ruth Anne still looked skeptical.

"Just follow me," Amy said. "We'll be back at the break area in half an hour."

They wound their way between bins of pillows, small-person play areas, countertops, info posts, and marketing banners hanging from the ceiling. Big impulse bins obscured corners, and at times Amy couldn't see the Bright and Shining Path through the maze of furniture. The massive Showroom floor receded to a vanishing point, warping and bending weirdly as it went, and after a while Amy felt as though she was wandering through a vast, trackless wasteland dotted with furniture from some vanished civilization.

They passed a row of six different Smagma bookshelves, each of them holding hundreds of copies of the same book (*Design Is Good*, orange and black dust jacket; Orsk bought them by the truckload), and then finally reached Kitchens, Amy's favorite part of the store. Her secret shame was that, after growing up with a two-burner hot plate and a toaster oven, she dreamed of having an Orsk kitchen.

She stopped in front of a gleaming all-white Harb-blo display and turned to Ruth Anne. "Could you imagine being able to afford something like that?"

Ruth Anne's breathing was shallow; a sheen of sweat glistened on her upper lip. She hunted through her pockets and pulled out a tube of Blistex. Applying it seemed to calm her breathing.

"I have that kitchen," she admitted. "Only my cabinets are slate gray instead of arctic white."

Amy felt stupid. Of course Ruth Anne could afford a nice kitchen. She wasn't drowning in loans for a college she'd dropped out of. She wasn't shopping for clothes at Goodwill. She probably had retirement investments and her car wasn't pissing oil all the time. As for Amy, she couldn't even conceive of paying for something that cost more than a hundred dollars.

"What's that noise?" Ruth Anne asked.

Amy listened. It was coming from the sink—something scratching on metal. She walked toward it.

"What is it?" Ruth Anne asked.

"Ergh!" Amy said, jerking back.

A plump black rat slithered bonelessly out of the drain. It scrabbled against the side of the sink and then its claws found purchase and it heaved itself up onto the counter. Ruth Anne clapped her hand over her mouth.

"What do we do?" Amy asked.

Both watched in horror as the rat waddled along the counter and then squeezed into the narrow gap between the refrigerator and the wall. They heard it slide down the drywall and plop onto the floor.

Ruth Anne grabbed Amy's wrist. "My feet!" she

exclaimed.

"What feet? Where?"

"I don't want it touching my feet!"

Ruth Anne darted up the Bright and Shining Path, and Amy followed. They had reached Dining Rooms before they stopped. Ruth Anne anxiously reapplied her Blistex.

"I've never seen a rat in here before," Amy said. "Basil is going to freak."

"The plumbing's not even hooked up," Ruth Anne said. "That means it was *inside* the cabinet. And rats are real social animals. Where there's one, there's always a dozen."

Amy shuddered, and they started walking again. The store felt endless, sprawled out around them all silent and secret, branching mazes and warrens full of furniture, like an infinite dollhouse. She tried to speed up, but Ruth Anne kept slowing down.

"Maybe we should go back and check Kitchens again," she said. "We came through there pretty fast. We might have missed somebody."

"Let's just keep going," Amy said.

They passed into Bedrooms, a vast plain of mattresses ringed with room displays. Ruth Anne stopped at one that showcased the Pykonne Collection.

"What about that closet?" she whispered. "Do you think we should check behind the door?"

"You think someone's hiding in there?"

The color drained from Ruth Anne's face. "Maybe?"

Amy walked over and yanked on the knob.

"Ah!" Ruth Anne squeaked prematurely.

"It's fake," Amy said, rattling the door, and the

display wall shook. "These doors to nowhere are all over the store. You really don't ever leave the checkout area, do you?"

Ruth Anne shook her head.

"Look at this," Amy said.

She reached behind a curtain and pulled the cord on a set of blinds. They rose to reveal four windowpanes made of cloudy white plastic screwed into the wall. "Amazing view, right?"

Ruth Anne had her eyes squeezed shut.

"It's okay," Amy said. "There's nothing to see. It's all fake."

Ruth Anne cracked open one eye, then both eyes, and looked embarrassed.

"I didn't want to see the Creepy Crawlies," she said.

Amy laughed. "The what?"

"When I was a little girl, I used to be scared of the dark," Ruth Anne said. "My parents moved me into my own bedroom, and I couldn't sleep for weeks. Every night I saw the Creepy Crawlies in the shadows. Nasty greasy dark stains on the wall, creeping down to get me. I couldn't tell anyone, but I had to do something. It wasn't enough to close my eyes, because I might peek. I thought if I couldn't see them, they couldn't see me. So I used to tie my socks around my head like a blindfold. Isn't that silly?"

"What would they do if they saw you?"

"I never found out," Ruth Anne said. Her voice got quiet. "Bad things."

The silence grew uncomfortable.

"Come on," Amy said. "You're freaking me out."

They continued walking, but Amy stuck a little

closer to Ruth Anne, mindful of the older woman's nerves. All this talk about Creepy Crawlies had her on edge, too.

The Showroom floor stretched off silently into the distance. They could hear the blowing of the big air movers up in the ceiling, but the music was turned off and the whole store had a sense of expectant listening. Behind them something cracked, and both women jumped.

"Keep going," Amy whispered.

They walked faster now. It took all of Amy's willpower not to run off wildly into the furniture, screaming and making noise so that some human sound would fill the vast emptiness. Abandoned aisles curled off the Bright and Shining Path like arms pointing the way into dead ends and cul-de-sacs, the ends of beds peered at them from doorways as they went by. They passed an information pillar, and wooden yardsticks hanging from a peg gently clacked together in the air conditioning. The rustle of their clothing felt too loud. The blood humming in their ears drowned out any sounds. Ruth Anne kept twisting around to make sure no one was behind them.

A movement caught Amy's eye.

Up ahead, something was squirming on a Müskk bed. A hairy ball writhed on the pillows like a nest of rats, and then it pinched itself in two, the shapes leaping off the bed and scrabbling backward. Amy blinked. She couldn't tell what she was seeing.

Then one of the shapes unfurled a limb and waved.

"Hey, guys, what's up?" Matt called.

Breathless, he wiped at his beard. On the other side of the bed, Trinity was pulling down her black

T-shirt.

"Hey," she said, red faced.

Ruth Anne let out a sob of relief and gripped Amy's arm.

"What the hell?" Amy asked.

"We're setting up base camp," Matt said.

"On a Müskk?" Amy asked, incredulous. "You broke into the store to hump on a filthy Müskk? Do you know how many kids have wiped their boogers on that thing?"

She sank down on the edge of a Sculpin display platform and started to laugh. Ruth Anne took a big ragged breath and started laughing, too. It felt good. It felt like a living thing to do in this sea of dead furniture. Trinity blushed, and Matt gave an embarrassed grin.

"We didn't break in," Trinity said after everyone settled down.

"Then how'd you get inside?" Amy asked.

"Hid in a couple of Liripips and waited for the floor to clear."

"So technically we didn't break into anything," Matt said.

"Basil is going to be pissed," Amy said.

"You can't tell Basil," Trinity said.

"Why?"

"He wouldn't understand. We're here to conduct a complete parapsychological investigation."

Amy and Ruth Anne just stared at her.

"In layman's terms," Matt explained, "we're ghost hunting. This place is teeming with potential paranormal energy, so we brought the necessary equipment to measure it." He gestured to four enormous black gear bags lying beside the bed. "MEL meters, infrared cameras, portable motion detectors, voice-activated recorders for EVP, the works."

"How'd you squeeze those into a Liripip?" Ruth Anne asked.

"They were out in the car," Matt said. "Once the coast was clear, we snuck down to the partners' entrance and brought them in."

"You're the ones who gummed the lock?" Amy asked. "We thought someone broke into the store. Basil has us doing floor sweeps. One loop around the Showroom every hour."

"Sucks to be you," Trinity said. "Once this breaks big, we'll be all sorry about it to Basil, but he'd never have authorized our shoot in the first place. Not with all the filming we're going to do."

"Now I get it," Ruth Anne said. "You're like the *Paranormal Investigators* on A&E."

"We are nothing like the *Paranormal Investigators* on A&E," Matt said. "For starters, we are not lame."

"But you have lots of equipment, just like the people on A&E," Ruth Anne pointed out.

"Stop saying A&E," Matt said. "We're aiming higher than that. Trinity wants us to be the first ghost hunters on Bravo."

"What happens when you find a ghost?" Ruth Anne asked.

"We get high-resolution footage," Trinity said. "No camera tricks, no CGI. Just real evidence of spiritual phenomena."

"And then?" Ruth Anne asked.

"If the ghost is up for a full Charlie Rose–style interview, we'll give it a shot," Matt said. "But I don't see that happening."

"You realize ghosts don't exist," Amy said.

"They do too exist," Trinity said. "Lots of people have seen them."

"Lots of people have seen Bigfoot," Amy said.

"Cryptozoology is a totally different area of research," Matt said. "Look, whether you believe in ghosts or not, you have to admit something strange is happening in this store. The broken Pronks, the help messages, the poop on the Brooka. Maybe it's not ghosts, but maybe it is." He tapped the floor with the toe of his boot. "Do you know what used to be here before they built Orsk?"

"Nothing," Ruth Anne said. "I used to drive past this place all the time and it was always just swamp-land."

"Before the swamp, there was a prison."

"I don't think so," Ruth Anne said.

"A long time ago," Trinity replied. "In the eigh-teenth century."

"Nineteenth," Matt said.

"What's the difference?" Trinity said.

"About a hundred years," Matt said. "It was pretty grim. A bunch of people died right where we're stand-ing and the jail sort of disappeared. Most people hav-en't even heard of it."

"That is spooky," Ruth Anne said.

"It's not spooky," Amy said. "It's not anything."

"Ignore the history if you want," Trinity said, hop-ping with excitement. "But all those people who died left behind psychic energy, and that's what's haunting the store. People used to get thrown in jail for stealing loaves of bread, so I bet their spirits are all pissed off."

She hoisted one of the massive gear bags onto the Müskk bed, unzipped it, and removed nine putty-colored plastic eggs. She arranged them in a line across the bedspread, cracked open a Valu-Pak of batteries, and began swapping in fresh nine-volts.

"What are those?" Ruth Anne asked.

"EMF readers," Trinity said. "I dropped in flash drives that time-stamp any spiking, so we can plot the changes over the course of the night."

"I don't know what any of that means," Ruth Anne said.

"Remember when everyone thought cell phones would give you brain cancer?" Trinity asked. "A bunch of cheapo electronics companies started making these so that people could see if electrical fields from their phones and power lines and stuff were floating through the air. Health nuts still use them, but mostly they're for ghost hunters."

"Because?" Amy asked.

"Because ghosts are energy," Trinity said. "Duh."

Amy turned to Matt. "You really believe this stuff?"

"It makes sense," he shrugged. "There's been a lot of research showing that electromagnetic fields caused by underground water or high-tension power lines induce haunting symptoms. People hear noises, they smell things, they get disoriented, they have mood swings. You can do it in a lab with a big magnet."

Trinity shook her head. "Ghosts *cause* electromagnetic activity, they aren't caused by electromagnetic activity."

"Have you ever seen one?" Amy asked.

"God, I want to," Trinity said. Her eyes were big.

"Wouldn't that be awesome? When I was a little kid, I used to watch horror movies when my parents weren't home and afterward I'd turn off all the lights and walk around in the dark trying to see a ghost. Matt says he saw one once. I'm totally jealous."

"You saw a ghost?" Ruth Anne asked Matt. "Was it scary?"

"Well, it could have been anything," Matt admitted. "It was just out of the corner of my eye."

"It was a ghost. A full-body apparition," Trinity insisted. "You told me."

"It was a long time ago," Matt said, with a sideways glance at Amy. "The point is, something strange is happening in this store. So we're going to shoot some footage, keep an open mind, see what we see."

"Because you know what those jerks on *Haunted Investigations*, *Paranormal Patrol*, *Strikeforce*: *Ghosts*, and *Ghost Detectives* never have?" Trinity asked. "Footage. They never actually get footage of a ghost. It's all just a bunch of fat dudes walking around dark houses going, 'Hello? Hello? I know you're here. I can feel your presence. Give me a sign.' Then they pretend to hear something and whip the camera around."

"Did you see that?" Matt imitated. "Did you hear that? Oh my God, it said, 'Help me.'"

"We're getting proof," Trinity said. "Tonight. On camera. And I don't mean orbs, or funnel ghosts, or swimmers, or ribbon energy. We're getting actual footage of actual apparitions. Then we're going to put our reel together, send it to 51 Minds or Antix or one of the other production companies, and they're going to flip. Boy-girl ghost-hunting teams are totally camera ready. Matt's going to bring the science and I'm going to bring the sparkle, and our reel is going to blow their minds and get us the hell out of Ohio. *Ghost Bomb*."

"What bomb?" Amy asked.

"*Ghost Bomb*," Trinity said. "It's the name of our show. Because it's about ghosts, and we're the bomb."

"Word," Matt said, high-fiving her.

Amy stared at them in disbelief. "That's the worst name I've ever heard."

Trinity scowled and extended a beautifully manicured middle finger.

"I think it's nice," Ruth Anne said. "*Ghost Bomb* sounds 'street.' Isn't that what they say?"

"Thank you," Trinity said before turning to Amy. "Now, I don't need you creeping around being all negative, because it's going to jinx us. Tonight is really important. I finally have an opportunity to get footage of a real live ghost. I don't need you and your negative energy chasing away the spirits." She turned back to Ruth Anne. "Why don't you come with me? You can help me put out the EMF meters. We'll get evidence of ghosts and be famous and awesome."

Trinity was not to be denied, and as soon as Ruth Anne had applied some Blistex she followed the girl back up the Bright and Shining Path, heading toward Dining Rooms. After a minute, they disappeared into the ranks of furniture, leaving Matt and Amy all alone.

MÜSKK

05

Retreat to a private island, where you can find the rest you need nesting in a cloud high above the cares of the world. **MÜSKK** envelops you in its caress and takes you on a journey into a land of dreams.

HEADBOARD IN NIGHT BEECH, BEAVER OAK, AND SYCAMORE
KING, QUEEN, AND TWIN SIZES AVAILABLE
ITEM NUMBER 7524321666

"Okay," said Matt, loading a backpack with EMF readers. "We need to put these all along the Bright and Shining Path."

"Do you really think they'll record anything?"

"Sure they will," Matt said. "Look at the size of the lighting grid."

He pointed at the ceiling. Twelve feet above their heads was a massive crisscrossed network of beams, pipes, wires, and huge HVAC ducts; everything was painted the same off-white color as the ceiling to help camouflage the infrastructure.

"Why do you want to detect the lighting grid?" Amy asked.

"I don't," Matt said. "But this store has six hundred eighty fill lights and another two hundred spotlights to hit accents, so it's generating most of the electromagnetic activity in the building. Which means that's what the meters are going to pick up."

He grabbed a meter and waved it in the air like

incense.

"Two milligauss," he said. "That's what it'll be reading all night long is my guess."

"Then why bother putting out the meters?"

Matt picked up a flip camera, slung a backpack over his shoulder, and handed Amy a store map and a pencil.

"Just mark down every place I leave one," he said. "Trinity will kill me if I lose any."

"But if they're not showing anything except the lighting grid," Amy asked, "then why are you putting them out?" She followed Matt down the Bright and Shining Path deeper into Bedrooms.

"Because that's Trinity's plan."

"And you're super in love with her?" she said.

Matt didn't answer. Amy knew the kind of effect Trinity had on male floor partners. All she had to do was act like a super-cute Japanese schoolgirl and she could recruit an entire army of ghost hunters.

Matt placed the first unit on a Sylbian bedside table. "Jason Hawes," he said. "My favorite Roto-Rooter employee."

Amy looked at him.

"I like to name the readers after TV ghost hunters," he explained. "Write them on the map, okay?"

They walked along the Bright and Shining Path, leaving Bedrooms and weaving through Bathrooms and Wardrobes. Matt stopped every seventy-five feet to place another meter atop a Finnimbrun chest of drawers, inside a Liripip ultranarrow single-door wardrobe, on top of a membership kiosk outside Children's. He named each one of them. "Lorraine Warren, chicken farmer . . . Ryan Buell, drama queen . . . Josh

Gates, adventure whore."

"What have you got against these people?" Amy asked.

"They jump to conclusions. They use the word *energy* without actually knowing what it means. They pretend to understand physics when they clearly don't even know how their own equipment works. They call themselves scientists but beat up the scientific method and drag it through the mud. And worst of all, they're terrible at being on TV."

"Whereas you guys would be awesome?"

"Obviously," Matt said. "Trinity has camera presence to burn. She's funny, she's got a great look, she's comfortable around tools, and she can solder a circuit, which is totally hot. Even if we don't get any apparitions on tape, we're still going to knock this out of the park. We'll chart the EMF spikes and drops, shoot in a bunch of different formats, like night-vision and infrared, record some suggestive electrovoice phenomena, use remote temperature probes to check cold spots, deploy motion detectors, and try to record any ultrasound we can find. When we're done, we'll have a buttload of awesome footage of the spookiest place on earth, which is this store, after hours, right now. Then I edit the hell out of it, and, ghost footage or no ghost footage, we're going to have a kickass reel."

It suddenly dawned on Amy.

"You don't believe in ghosts," she said. "At all."

Matt powered up his camera. "I believe a ghost is a subjective experience. It doesn't have an objective reality. It exists solely in the perceptions of the people who see it."

"Meaning, ghosts aren't real?"

"That's not what I said. Come on, let's roll tape. It's like outtakes from *Child's Play* in here."

They had arrived in Children's, and Amy watched as Matt directed the camera at stuffed animals stacked in big impulse bins like dead bodies, shelves of vacant-eyed dolls staring idiotically off into the distance, circus animal sheets stretched across never-used beds, kids' bedrooms abandoned in a haunted city. Matt wasn't dumb. After watching every season of every ghost-hunting show ever created, he knew exactly how to give an audience what it wanted: creepy dolls, spooky rooms, and the eerie framing of ambiguous shadows.

"You told Trinity you witnessed a ghost firsthand. A full-body apparition. That's what she said."

"I saw *something* my brain perceived to be a ghost," Matt said. "But the mind is a complicated place. Temporal-lobe seizures, sleep paralysis, pareidolia; it could have been anything."

"Except the soul of a dead person searching for the light."

"Exactly."

They took the shortcut over to Storage Solutions, Matt stopping to lie on the floor and frame a Runcate looming over him, crawling up on top of a Qualtagh and getting an overhead shot of the silent ranks of furniture. He panned along a Plexiglas display case; inside, a mechanical arm dumbly opened and closed the door of a Yclept media cabinet over and over to demonstrate the strength and durability of Orsk hinges.

"Trinity thinks ghosts are real," Amy said. "But your whole ghost thing is just a ploy to get into her pants."

"Why do you care whether Trinity and I are hooking up?" Matt asked. "Do you see me grilling you about your sex life?"

"Because it's further proof that guys are dogs," Amy said. "This obviously means a lot to Trinity, and you're pretending you believe in it to trick her into sleeping with you. That's some deep craziness. Did you make up the story about the prison, too?"

"The Cuyahoga Panopticon was a real place," Matt said. "You've never heard of it?"

"I don't have a strong grasp of Ohio's extraordinary history."

"It was a big deal back in the nineteenth century. The warden—Josiah Worth—was a total maniac. He believed that nonstop surveillance would 'cure' criminals. The prison was round, with a guardhouse in the center, so that the prisoners—he called them penitents—never knew if they were being watched. Zero privacy. It was called a panopticon. Underneath the cells were three sub-basements where the penitents worked. Giant labyrinths full of mindless tasks designed to rewire their brains." He shrugged. "Just like Orsk."

"Don't let Basil hear you say that."

"But it's true," Matt protested. "Orsk is all about scripted disorientation. The store wants you to surrender to a programmed shopping experience. The Cuyahoga Panopticon was the same thing. The warden believed he could cure a criminal brain using forced labor, mindless repetition, and total surveillance. This was back when people believed that architecture could be designed to generate a psychological effect."

Matt led Amy past a row of gleaming white Helvetesniks, and they took the shortcut to Wardrobes.

They emerged to find themselves standing in front of a Plexiglas display case. Inside, a mechanical arm dumbly opened and closed the door of a Yclept media cabinet over and over to demonstrate the strength and durability of Orsk hinges.

Somehow they'd traveled in a circle.

"Weren't you paying attention to where we were going?" Amy asked.

"I was monologuing," Matt said. "But this basically proves my point. If you lose your focus in this store for even a moment, you're lost. Get distracted and the next thing you know, you're dropping eight hundred bucks on a fiberboard Runcate."

They returned to the Bright and Shining Path and followed the arrows that would lead them back to Kitchens, Dining Rooms, and, ultimately, Bedrooms.

"You'd think I'd have this place figured out by now," Matt said.

"Sure," Amy said dryly. "Sounds like you've got your whole life figured out."

"Not my life," Matt said. "Just my Escape from Ohio plan. *Ghost Bomb* is going to be huge, me and Trinity will live happily ever, and the next time you're channel-surfing on Bravo, you'll—dammit!"

Both Matt and Amy stopped. They had arrived in a sea of birch, black, and white tabletops, desks, and rolling swivel chairs. Somehow they'd walked *backward* into Home Office.

"See what I mean?" Matt said. "Our great lord and master, Tom Larsen, built his stores to induce the

Gruen Transfer: a sense of confusion and geographic despair that keeps you completely disoriented. Like Ikea or Crate and Barrel. Heck, I got lost in a Sam's Club last week."

"I get it," Amy said. "You've made your point."

Matt's cell phone rang and he checked the display. "Trinity," he said. He answered the phone, agreed to meet her back at the Müskk, and hung up. "They're waiting for us."

Amy thought only a few minutes had passed, but when she checked her watch she realized nearly half an hour had gone by. Basil would be wondering what had happened.

They reversed course on the Bright and Shining Path, for a third time heading back toward Kitchens and Dining Rooms. "I need to get Ruth Anne and head back to the break area," Amy said. "What do you want me to tell Basil?"

"What do you mean?"

"When he hears you guys sneaked into the store, he's going to be pissed."

Matt didn't answer. He was staring through his camera viewfinder, bewildered. They rounded the corner into what should have been Kitchens and found themselves once again facing Home Office.

"Wait, what just happened?" Amy asked.

Matt shook his head. "This doesn't make any sense."

"You walked in another circle."

"Look at the camera."

Amy looked as Matt pointed the lens down the Bright and Shining Path into Home Office.

The screen was showing Kitchens.

"That's the footage from earlier," Amy said.

"No," Matt said, panning the camera. Every time he moved, the view of Kitchens moved with him. He zoomed forward until the screen was filled with a Gradgrind cabinet system. He got so close that Amy could read the SKU and sale price.

But in front of the lens, there in reality, was only empty air.

"It's a problem with the memory card," Amy said.

Matt ejected the card and held it between his fingers, like a magician revealing the one you picked. "It's not a problem with the card."

"I refuse to accept this," Amy said.

"Accept it or not," Matt said, "we are both experiencing it, so we have three choices. Either what's in front of us really is Kitchens, but we think it's Home Office, and the camera is right. Or what's in front of us is Home Office, but for some reason the camera is showing us Kitchens, so the camera is wrong."

"What's the third choice?"

"We're both losing our minds."

"This is impossible," Amy said, feeling helpless.

"It's *very* possible," Matt said. "Remember what I told you about EM fields? The really strong ones mess with your brain. Maybe it's the lighting grid, maybe it's power lines, maybe there's a giant geomagnetic field under the building."

"If it's affecting our brains," Amy said, "then why is it also affecting your camera?"

"Maybe it's not," Matt said. "Maybe the camera is fine, and both of us are hallucinating that it's not."

Eventually they settled on a new tactic: this time they would navigate using what was on the screen, ignoring the reality of their surroundings. Matt panned the camera until the tiny screen showed them the direction they wanted to go, then he held it up in front of them. They followed the path on the screen, ignoring what was actually around them. The split perception made Amy feel like she was going to be sick.

"I don't want to go crazy," she said.

"We're not going crazy," Matt said. "We're experiencing some rather extreme effects of electromagnetic fields on the human brain."

They followed the camera, and the route took them in a crazy looping circle through reality. On the screen, they were walking through Storage Solutions. In real life, they were colliding with wastebaskets and file cabinets in Home Office, then climbing over ottomans and end tables in Living Rooms.

"What happens if we make it back to the Müskk, but we don't see Ruth Anne and Trinity?" Amy asked. "What happens if they're on the screen but not in real life?"

"One freaky crisis at a time," Matt said. "To your left, watch out."

He pushed Amy's head down and she narrowly missed braining herself on the edge of a display shelf. They crawled over a Potemkin armchair and then out the other side of the room display. On the camera's screen they were taking a hard right-hand turn.

"That's sending us back the way we came," Amy said.

"Don't panic," Matt advised. "Just follow the camera."

Amy placed one hand on Matt's shoulder and kept

going, both of them walking faster now. Their breathing was shallow and Matt was sweating through his hoodie. They rounded the last corner, and in one disorienting blur, the image onscreen and the image in front of them blended together as one.

Trinity and Ruth Anne were sitting on a Müskk, waiting.

"Where were you guys?" Trinity asked. "Making out?"

Amy sat on the edge of the bed, clutching the sides of her head, trying to steady her thoughts. "I don't even know how to explain it," she said. "We were lost. We were absolutely, completely disoriented."

"That's a tiny bit of an exaggeration," Matt said. "I got us back here, didn't I?"

Ruth Anne knelt beside Amy, concerned. "You do look a little peaky. What happened?"

Amy recounted everything she and Matt had just experienced, explaining how they'd used the viewfinder to guide their way back to Bedrooms. As the story progressed, Trinity grew more and more excited.

"Sounds like paranormal activity to me," she said. "What else could it be? There's no rational explanation."

"There are plenty of rational explanations," Matt said.

"Rational, shmational, I want to try it," Trinity said. "Get the camera and let's go to Kitchens, see if we can make it happen again." She grabbed Matt's hand and pulled him down the Bright and Shining Path. He scarcely had time to snag a gear bag.

Amy turned to Ruth Anne. "We need to get back to the break room. Basil will be waiting for us."

"Of course," Ruth Anne said, wrapping an arm around Amy's waist and helping her off the bed. "Come on, hon. Maybe you just need something from the vending machine. Some pretzels to get your blood sugar back up."

Together they headed into Wardrobes, and the great Showroom silence settled over them like a shroud. Amy told herself she wasn't scared anymore, but as they walked along the Path, she was increasingly certain they were lost again. She picked up her pace, panic crawling up her spine, and then a massive wave of relief washed over her when at last up ahead she finally saw the brightly colored bunk beds of Children's. Even then, she wouldn't allow herself to relax until she and Ruth Anne were back in the break area, all four walls clearly visible and close enough to touch.

"I'm glad that's over," Ruth Anne said quietly.

"Me, too."

"And according to Basil's schedule, we get a fifteen-minute break before starting the next patrol."

Amy's heart sank.

KJËRRING 06

A way to browse your memory, **KJËRRING** brings order and organization to your favorite books, movies, music . . . everything that adds beauty, elegance, and art to your life.

AVAILABLE IN NATURAL BEECH, LIGHT BEECH, AND KHAKI
W 57¾ X D 18¼ X H 52¼
ITEM NUMBER 7766611132

Basil was furious when Amy and Ruth Anne returned to the break room. "What part of 'thirty minutes' did you not understand?" he asked. "What have you been doing?"

"Talking to Matt and Trinity," Ruth Anne explained.

"What?" Basil said.

"They're the ones who gummed up the partners' entrance," Ruth Anne said. "But Trinity told me they'd clean it up before they left, so you don't have to worry about that."

"What?" Basil repeated.

"They're over in Bedrooms," Ruth Anne said. "But it's okay, they're not vandalizing anything. They're just filming a video for their ghost-hunting show."

"What?" Basil asked again.

"You know how on A&E they've got those ghost hunters?" Ruth Anne said. "Oh, shoot, they don't want to be on A&E, though. Right, it's Bravo. Anyway, they say this place is built on an old prison and they've got cameras and microphones and all kinds of electromagnetic detectors and they're shooting their own little ghost show. It's real cute. We caught them kissing, didn't we, Amy?"

"We did," Amy said, sitting down on one of the Arsles and crossing her arms over her chest.

She decided that she was going to sit there and definitely, absolutely not go back out on the floor for the rest of the night. She resisted the urge to check her phone. The last time she'd looked it had been 12:20. She thought if she checked again and it wasn't at least 1 a.m. she would go crazy.

She *couldn't* check it again.

It felt too soon to check it again.

But finally, against her better judgment, she checked it again.

Twelve twenty-five a.m.

"This is unbelievable," Basil said. "Why would they do this?"

"They want to make Orsk famous," Ruth Anne said.

"It's already famous," Basil said. "You need to show me where they are. Right now."

Amy didn't want to get involved. She wanted to just sit in the corner where things were sane and not go back out onto the floor. Trying to find somewhere to rest her eyes, she glanced up.

"Was that stain always there?" she asked, studying a faded yellow blotch that covered three of the ceiling tiles.

"Yes," Basil said.

"I don't think it was," she said.

"It's faded," Basil pointed out. "So it can't be new. Mystery solved."

Amy had a nagging sense that he was wrong. Earlier in the evening, when he was quoting from chapter three of *Some Assembly Required: My Life in Retail* by Tom Larsen, Amy could remember rolling her eyes toward the heavens and counting the ceiling tiles. She had counted to one hundred twelve before stopping, and none of them had been stained.

"Let's go," Basil said. "I need to deal with this Matt and Trinity situation."

"It's hardly a situation," Ruth Anne said.

"Yes, it is," Basil said. "It is most *definitely* a situation."

But before they could take further action, the situation came clattering down the hall to them. Trinity burst through the door, whooping loudly, waving a camera in one hand.

"I got a ghost!" She ran around the break room, leaping, swinging her arms wildly, waving them over her head, dancing backward. "I got a ghost! I got a ghost! I got a ghosty, ghosty, ghosty ghost!"

"Stop!" Basil shouted. "You are way out of line! You shouldn't even be here!"

"It's not a ghost," Matt panted, arriving in the doorway, dripping with sweat. "Someone got through the partners' entrance. He's here in the store with us. Right now."

"You guys can't do this," Basil said. "You can't just run around and act crazy. There are liability issues. If Pat knew about this, he'd fire you on the spot."

"We can show him my footage," Trinity said. "Because I got footage and it's *amazing*."

"It was not a ghost," Matt repeated. "Ghosts don't—that's not how they work."

"Stop it!" Basil shouted, and this time Trinity finally stopped dancing. "I am not in the mood. Tomorrow morning, after Corporate leaves, we are going to have a serious coaching about your future at Orsk."

"My future is *Ghost Bomb*," Trinity told him. "Because we are definitely getting green-lit with this footage. It is going to blow your mind."

"Well, I don't know about anyone else," Ruth Anne said, "but I'd like to see it."

"You're embarrassing yourself," Matt said to Trinity. "It's not a ghost. Someone is hiding in the store."

"The only person who's going to be embarrassed is you," Trinity said. "I know it's a ghost because I saw him and he went right by me and I got him on tape. You don't think he's a ghost because you're a jealous butthole."

"Ghosts don't exist," Matt snapped. "They've never existed. They didn't exist yesterday, they don't exist today, and they're not going to exist tomorrow. They're made-up bedtime stories for mouth-breathers who are scared of dying and you're too smart to believe in them!"

His statement hung in the air like something that absolutely, positively could not be taken back. Trinity looked as though she'd been slapped.

"I mean," Matt said, stammering, "I guess they *could* exist, but I don't think this was one."

"Screw off," Trinity said, turning her back on him. "You want to see my ghost, Ruth Anne? Come here and take a look."

Trinity had the camera open and was rewinding the footage. Against her better judgment Amy drifted over to watch. Lines of static crackled, and then the film slowed to normal speed. On the screen was one of the EMF meters, sitting in the middle of the massive slab of a Frånjk dining room table surrounded by eight chairs. The shot zoomed out until the EMF meter was just a little white dot, then the camera moved toward it, generating a slasher-movie point-of-view effect as it rocked from side to side.

Trinity's voice, tinny and electronic, squeaked out of the camera's speaker. "The punishments of the penitents were designed to redeem their souls. Even today, this Orsk superstore echoes with the cries of the dead."

"Are you narrating?" Amy asked.

"I told her not to do that," Matt said.

"No one's listening to you, Matt," Trinity said.

The camera panned across the room display as it approached the dining table. It passed one of the "Orsk: Our Home Is Forever" posters that listed all the environmentally friendly materials used to make the Frånjk line. It panned past a human figure standing in the bedroom door. Then it panned past a set of Rimmeyob shelves. Around her, Amy felt everyone stop breathing. Her legs went numb.

Slowly, the camera panned back toward the bedroom door, but it was too late. A shadow rushed out and the lens went black. The camera rocked up and flipped over, and light fixtures streaked across the frame.

"Did you see?" Trinity exclaimed. "He came right at me! He was freezing cold and brushed past me, and

I tripped over one of the chairs."

"He *jumped* you," Matt said.

"He was trying to communicate!" Trinity said.

The footage did a flip and suddenly they were looking at the back of a man running down the Path toward Kitchens. Amy caught a glimpse of a dark blue shirt and white tennis shoes before he dove behind an island countertop.

"You see?" Matt asked. "He's wearing sneakers. What kind of ghost wears sneakers?"

"Oh, my God," Amy said. "I've seen this guy! He was here this morning when I got to work. I saw him standing in Bedrooms."

"Why didn't you say anything?" Basil asked.

"Because I'm not Loss Prevention, okay?" Amy said. "It's not my job."

"'See Something, Say Something,'" Basil said. "It's right there on page thirty-six of the employee handbook. You should know better, Amy."

Amy ignored him. "This is the guy," she said. "The graffiti in the bathroom. The poop on the Brooka. This is totally the guy!"

"He's not a guy," Trinity said. "He's a ghost."

"He's not a ghost!" Matt said.

Trinity turned on him. "Have you been lying to me this entire time? You said you believed in ghosts—but now that I've finally got clear footage, you say he's *not* a ghost?"

"Have you even been listening to what I've been saying?" Matt asked.

"No," Trinity said. "Because everything you've said has been quitter talk. We came here to shoot footage of ghosts and we are not leaving until we shoot footage of ghosts. The end."

"Both of you! Stop it!" Basil shouted.

His voice echoed off the walls of the tiny room. Everyone stopped.

"This is not a slumber party!" he snapped. "I've got two partners who broke a lock to film a TV show in my store. I've got a vandal writing graffiti and defecating on furniture. And in"—he checked his watch—"six hours, a Consultant Team is showing up and this place has to look pristine, this situation has to be resolved, and Pat has to get a clean bill of health from Regional, or we will all be submitting our résumés to the Ikea in Pittsburgh. Do you understand?"

Everyone silently took in his assessment.

"First things first," Basil said. "We find this guy."

"This *ghost*," Trinity said.

"Not a ghost," Matt hissed back.

"Cut it out," Basil said. "We're going to stick together and we're going to scour the store from one end to the other. And when we find him, we're going to figure out what to do with him. And then I'm going to figure out what to do with the two of you."

"How're you going to find him?" Amy asked.

"I don't know," Basil said. "Maybe we form a line and walk the store in a grid."

"There he is," said Trinity.

"Or we start in the center and walk out in widening circles," Matt said.

"He's right there," Trinity said.

"Maybe if we got up high, we could look over the walls and get a better view of the store and break it down into sectors and do it that way," Basil said.

"Or we could go where he is," Trinity said.

"And you know that *how*?" Basil asked, annoyed.

"Because I'm looking at him," Trinity said.

They all turned to follow her gaze.

The flat-screen TV hanging in the corner had been tuned to CNN, but now it was showing footage shot on a consumer-model video camera. The image was blown-out and blurry, with no CNN logos or news crawls. It appeared to be the feed from a security camera. The image was underlit, but it was definitely showing the Showroom floor, somewhere on the border between Bedrooms and Dining Rooms.

"There," Trinity said, walking over and touching the screen.

They all saw it. Sticking out from around the side of a Kjërring shelving unit was a man's leg. All they could see were his pants from the knee down, a bare ankle, and a dirty sneaker. While they watched, his leg slipped out of sight behind the Kjërring. The movement was so startling that Amy took a step back. Everyone looked at Basil. In the face of something so unsettling, they needed a leader. Basil sensed the change and rose to the occasion.

"Okay," he said. "We're going to Dining Rooms."

"How'd security footage get on TV?" Amy asked.

"I have no idea," Basil said. "But as far as unanswered questions go, that's way down on my list. Right now, we've got someone in the store and we need to go . . . talk to him. See who it is. You know, deal with this."

"Just give me a second to swap batteries," Trinity said, opening her backpack.

"You aren't coming," Basil said.

"Not a chance," Trinity said.

"He's right, Trinity," Matt said. "This guy already

came at you once. Let us handle him."

"You're not coming, either," Basil said.

"Ha!" Trinity laughed.

"You can't lock us in here," Matt said. "There's not even a door."

"Then we'll escort you to your vehicle," Basil said.

"We need to get our stuff. It's expensive."

Basil looked very tired.

"Excuse me," Ruth Anne said, "I don't mean to stick my nose in your business, but maybe we should go find this man before he hides again? And there is safety in numbers. Maybe we should all stick together for now?"

"How long ago did you shoot this footage?"

"About fifteen minutes," Matt said.

"All right," Basil said. "We're sticking together until we find this guy. And bring your camera in case we need to document anything for Pat. Just to prove I did everything correctly."

Moments later the group followed Basil out of the break room. Amy didn't want to go out on the floor, but she didn't want to be alone, either. She split the difference by hanging back as far as possible.

Basil stopped outside the women's restroom.

"You said something about graffiti?" he asked.

"It's inside," she said.

They all followed Basil into the bathroom, with Amy bringing up the rear. For a moment, none of them could even speak. The walls were covered with scratches, as if someone had taken a chisel and carved them from floor to ceiling. Every inch of the industrial yellow paint was marked, chipped, chopped, scratched, gouged, defaced.

Archie WILSON   Carson Moore/Beehive
BEEHIVE   here   3 YR   6 YR   J. BUXTON
3 years   IS   4 YR   7 YR   BEEHIVE
    forever   5 YR   FOREVER   2 YR.

ghegan   danny dye
                    1 year and
Paddy the PIG   BILL Poole   VI   2 year
⑤ YEAR   Dolph Saunders   Charley Lozier   ARCHIBALD
    1st day 2nd day 3rd day   six   various years
    GALLUS Mag   eight for my lord   various years
                    (10 years)
Singer   '39   Ikey Vail   MIKE Byrnes
tolenbaum   four more   1827   8 YEARS
years 3 year

Gentleman Joe   Harry Hilton   Dassle Dr
4 YR 5 YR   5 year?
                Paudeen McLaughlin
ANNY   Billy McGlory   NEVER
    2 Y
    Gaylord B. Hubbell   DANNY DRISCO
    I II III IIII IIII VII   1 year
                    III years
III KIT BOERER   Old JUNK   Fernando
BEEHIVE   IIIIIIIIIII   Fernando Woo
2 years
5 YR   three y

Cox/beehive
3 yr
5 yr
6 yr
7 yr
Beezey Garrity
'31 — '38 R.I.P.
BEEHIVE
Tom Gould
IV
1833
Slobbery Jim
Dan Noble
forever
Never
band
for eternal rest
Louis the Eyes
1 year
6 years
2 year
4 YEAR
Owney Geog
III
Shad Belly
1 y
2 y
6 y
Lazarus
HELL HERE
DUTCH Heinrichs,
until My Jesus brings me Home
Jesus loves me
gentle and wild
bless me Jesus
forgive me Jesus
MICK THE JUDGE
1 YEAR
+ 1 YEAR MORE
traveling Jack
TONY McNally
YANCY RAWLS
Beehive
6 MONTHS
2 years
3 years
4 years
5 years
QUIMBO
3 ye
the hurt stop hurt
IT Burns
YEAR hard
BILLY PATTERSON
6 year
'38
Tom Hyer
'29 – '33

"This is . . . " Basil trailed off. "Why didn't you say something?"

"It wasn't this bad," Amy said. "It's gotten worse."

Trinity ran her fingers over the wall in wonder. Ruth Anne stood very, very still, trying to avoid touching anything. The bathroom smelled like the Brooka, only worse.

"Beehive," Matt read aloud. The word was repeated over and over, along with countless names and numbers. "What the hell is a Beehive?"

"There's no way one person did this," Basil said. "Not since the store closed. This would have taken all night."

And yet there it was, right in front of them.

"I can't breathe this smell anymore," Ruth Anne said, leaving the restroom. The others followed her out to the hallway.

"I'm sure there's a reasonable explanation," Basil said. "I want everyone to listen and do exactly what I say. Do you all understand?"

"We need to call the police," Amy said.

"Definitely not," Basil said. "If the police come, Pat comes. He'll be mad, Corporate still shows up in the morning, and the problem isn't solved. But if we go through the store together, if we find this guy, we can fix the problem once and for all."

"I'm not going back to the Showroom," Amy said. "I'm sorry, but one floor sweep was enough for me."

"Suit yourself," Basil said. "You and Ruth Anne can stay in the break area. Going forward, I don't want anyone alone in the store."

Ruth Anne nodded, but she didn't look happy about it.

"Call my cell phone if you see anything suspicious," Basil said. "And whatever happens, do not leave the break room. There are enough people running around in here. It's starting to feel like an episode of *Scooby-Doo*. We'll regroup when we find this guy."

It was the first time all night that Amy was glad to follow Basil's orders. She walked back to the break room and took out her cell phone.

"I don't like this," Ruth Anne said, coming in after her.

"Me, either," Amy said, tapping her phone's screen.

"What're you doing?"

"Calling the cops."

"But we just said we weren't going to do that."

"I lied."

"Nine one one, what is your emergency?" the operator asked.

"Hi, I'm at the Cuyahoga Orsk and we've got a customer or someone hiding in the store. He's vandalized our bathroom, and I think he's dangerous."

"Do you want police, fire, or emergency?"

"Police, I guess? A police emergency?"

"Is anyone injured?"

"No, but he scared the hell out of everyone."

"And what is your exact location?"

"I'm at Orsk. The furniture store. Off Route 77, near Independence."

"Do you have an exact street address?"

Amy's mind went blank. She never thought of Orsk as having an address—it was always just *there*, plopped down on the side of the highway, like a Cracker Barrel or a Home Depot. She searched the memos tacked to the employee bulletin board for some kind of street address. Finally she found one buried in the fine print on Orsk letterhead.

"Seventy-four fourteen River Park Drive. That's the feeder road right off Route 77," she told the operator.

"And is that a residence or a business?"

"Amy?" Ruth Anne mouthed.

"It's a business. It's a giant building with a giant sign screaming 'Orsk' in giant ten-foot letters. There's like a hundred of them across the country. You know?"

"Amy?" Ruth Anne whispered, tapping her on the shoulder.

"Hold on," Amy said to the dispatcher and held the phone against her stomach. "What?"

"Hang up the phone."

"Why?"

"I need this job. You're young and you can go somewhere else, but I can't. If I lose this job, I won't get another one. Hang up."

"Who cares about your job? What about your safety?"

"I'm begging you, Amy. As your friend. Please hang up."

Amy hesitated for a moment, then raised the phone back to her ear.

"Ma'am?" the dispatcher said. "Are you there?"

"Listen, I made a mistake," Amy said. "We don't need the police."

"Ma'am, I already have units on the way. I have to—"

Amy hung up.

"Thank you," Ruth Anne said.

"This is a bad idea," Amy said. "Basil's making it worse, not better."

"He'll find the man and it'll all be fine," Ruth Anne said. "I know it will be. Calling the police just undermines his authority."

Amy's cell phone rang. She answered.

"Ma'am, I lost your call." It was the 911 operator calling her back. "I want you to know that we have a unit on the way to your location, 7414 River Park Drive, from Brecksville. They should be there shortly."

"Thank you," Amy said. She hung up and turned to Ruth Anne. "They're coming anyways."

"Oh," Ruth Anne said, chewing her lip. "Well."

"I'm sorry," Amy said. "But you know what? I'm not *that* sorry. Let's just sit here quietly, and in twenty minutes it'll all be over."

"No," Ruth Anne said. "We're going to go upstairs and we're going to help Basil find this person before the police get here. We're going to do what he says, and we're going to keep our jobs."

"Not me. I am not going back on that floor."

"Oh, boy," Ruth Anne said. She looked nervously around the room as though she was checking to see if anyone was watching. Then she looked back at Amy and all the hesitation, all the nervousness, all the nicey-nice that made her Ruth Anne was gone. "Listen to me, you spoiled child."

Amy had never heard Ruth Anne talk this way. She didn't know Ruth Anne *could* talk this way.

"Maybe you've got a safety net, but I don't. I don't have a family, I don't have a lot of friends, and when I'm home at night, I usually spend my time doing crosswords and watching TV with Snoopy. You know who Snoopy is? He's the stuffed dog I won at the Great Lakes Fair. Now, you know what I do have? This job. It pays my rent, it gives me a family, it bought me a beautiful kitchen, and I am not going to lose it because some little girl who thinks it's her job to lip off all the time has the willies and won't go upstairs to help her coworkers find the person sneaking around this store."

"Ruth Anne—"

"No, you've talked plenty tonight. Now it's time for you to listen. The last time I checked you were twenty-four years old. Thirteen and angry is a long way back in your rearview mirror. You need to buckle up because it is time to toe the line and act like a grown-up woman. You don't want to go out on the floor? Tough titty, said the kitty. I don't want to go on the floor, either, but having a job is all about doing things you don't want to do. That's why they pay you money for it. Life doesn't care what you want, other people don't care what you want. All that matters is what you do. And right now, what you're going to do is stand shoulder to shoulder with me and march out that door, find our friends, and help them deal with this situation. Tomorrow you can do whatever the heck you want, but I am going to keep my job. So get up, put some pepper in your pants, and let's get moving."

Amy opened her mouth to say something but then realized she didn't have a single thing to say except "Okay."

ORSK EMPLOYEE EVALUATIONS

STORE NUMBER: 00108   **STORE LOCATION:** Cuyahoga, Ohio   **SUPERVISOR:** Basil Washington

EMPLOYEE ID:	NAME:	SHOP:	TERM:
408 2156800	Trinity Park	Staging and Design	3 years

EVALUATION:

Store Partner's engagement with customers on supernatural issues has required two Face-to-Face Coachings, but her Staging solutions continue to create an inspiring retail environment. Effective leadership is defined by results, not attributes.

EMPLOYEE ID:	NAME:	SHOP:	TERM:
407 2345641	Matthew C. McGrath	Living Rooms & Sofas	4 years

EVALUATION:

This Store Partner seems to be suffering from the delusion that every conversation about facial hair grooming requires him to invoke the First Amendment. I am not sure this Store Partner understands the meaning of the First Amendment. No Coaching is recommended. The key to successful management is leadership, not authority.

EMPLOYEE ID:	NAME:	SHOP:	TERM:
408 2156759	Amy Porter	Home Office	3 years

EVALUATION:

This Store Partner has demonstrated a poor comprehension of the duties required for being Shop Responsible; however, I believe that she has the potential to move into management. Suggest striking results of her Shop Responsible test, and I will prepare her to retake the test in six weeks. The function of leadership is to produce more leaders, not more followers.

EMPLOYEE ID:	NAME:	SHOP:	TERM:
405 1110627	Ruth Anne DeSoto	Checkout	14 years

EVALUATION:

I recommend again that this Store Partner receive a promotion and pay raise. In reviewing her record, I have noticed that she has not received a compensation increase in three years. I feel that a Tier 1 increase in her compensation will demonstrate Orsk's appreciation of her long service. Make your top retail partners rich, and they will make you rich.

WANWEIRD

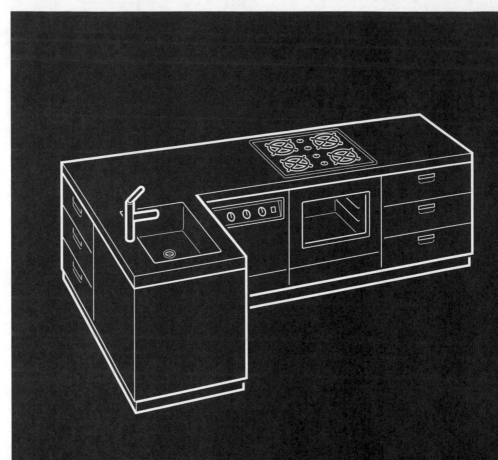

The heart of the home is your kitchen, where good cooking, good smells, good food, and good friends flow. **WANWEIRD** provides a contemporary look that empowers you to create your next work of art, whether it's breakfast for two or dinner for twelve.

AVAILABLE IN SNOW, NIGHT, AND SLATE
SIZES WILL VARY DEPENDING UPON YOUR CONFIGURATION
FOR FURTHER INFORMATION, JUST ORSK!

They found Basil and the others in Bedrooms, hiding behind a Drazel chest of drawers.

"Shhhh," Matt hissed, waving them over. "The guy's . . . in . . . there."

He jabbed a finger toward the double doors leading to the back of house. Amy obediently ducked behind the Drazel.

"What'd he look like?" she whispered.

"We didn't actually see him," Basil said. "But Trinity saw someone moving and then we all saw the doors swinging. We're going to lure him out, then we'll nab him in a pincer movement."

"What's a pincer movement?" Amy asked.

"Oh, for Pete's sake," Ruth Anne said. She marched up to the double doors and pushed them wide open. "There's nobody here. He's probably still in Dining Rooms hiding under some shelves, the poor thing."

"That was extremely dangerous," Basil said. "You could have been attacked."

Ruth Anne shook her head. "Anyone hiding in this store is probably in a heap of trouble. My guess is that this fella needs some serious help."

"She's got a point," Amy said. "I don't want to be here. Why would this guy?"

Basil ignored her. "Let's go to Dining Rooms."

"Hang on," Matt said.

He opened a Tawse wardrobe and removed one of his gear bags. He unzipped the top, reached inside, and pulled out a black Maglite. It was about two feet long and resembled a cross between a flashlight and a riot baton. It looked like it could put a serious crease in a skull.

"You are not going to use that on a human being," Basil said.

"That depends," Matt said. "This guy nearly attacked Trinity."

"I've been trained in retail crisis management," Basil said. "Let me handle this."

Matt marched off toward Dining Rooms without answering him. "You can't beat up a ghost," Trinity called, going after him, the others following in their wake.

"You do realize that you're not in control of this situation anymore," Amy said to Basil.

"I am one hundred percent in control of this situation," Basil said, hurrying to keep up.

They began the long trip along the Bright and Shining Path to Dining Rooms. They passed enormous Pronk mirrors leaning against the walls and showing cold, silver versions of themselves trapped in glass. They walked past rows of armchairs waiting for visitors who would never come, past stripped shelves, bare tables, empty beds, doors to nowhere.

"Something smells," Ruth Anne said.

"Something nasty," Trinity added.

The sour, marshy stench of rotten mud crept across the Showroom floor like a low-lying fog. The closer they got to Dining Rooms the worse it got, crawling up their nostrils and creeping down their throats. It was the same smell in the bathroom, the same smell emanating from the Brooka earlier that morning. It made Amy's skin feel slimy.

"Stay close," Matt told Trinity, but she pulled away from him, still angry.

Finally they arrived at the dining room display they'd seen on the security camera. They stopped on the edge of the Bright and Shining Path, feeling as if they had just stepped onto a television set and were now being watched by an invisible audience of millions. The chairs from the Frånjk collection were tipped on their sides, and a plastic EMF reader sat in the center of the massive Frånjk table. Amy's heart was pounding.

"Spirits, can you hear me?" Trinity called.

"Sssh!" Matt snapped. "Don't call attention to yourself."

"Don't tell me what to do," Trinity snapped back. She was aiming her camera into every corner, trying to get another look at her ghost. "Spirits, reveal yourselves!"

"I just don't believe this," Ruth Anne said. "I'm a bigger 'fraidy cat than all of you, but this is ridiculous." She got down on her knees and peered underneath the Kjërring storage unit. "Nothing again. He's gone."

Amy felt doubly relieved. Maybe now they would go back to the break room. Even better, maybe they'd call it a night and go home. But then she glanced across the Bright and Shining Path, and she saw it.

On the other side of the walkway, opposite Dining Rooms, was a purple Sylbian bedroom display. Everything in the room was meticulously arranged. Not a single detail was out of place—except the ruffled white bed skirt around the box spring. Underneath it, protruding from the shadows, rested a hairy human hand with a gold wedding band on one finger.

Amy nudged Basil. He followed her jabbing finger, and his eyes went cartoon-character wide.

Their terrified focus alerted Matt and he turned around, followed both their gazes, and took an involuntary half step backward when he saw the hand. He tried to pull Trinity back, but she squirmed out of his grip. Ruth Anne retreated on tiptoes to the opposite side of the Bright and Shining Path.

"Um, we see you," Basil announced, too loudly.

Nothing happened.

"Under the bed," he continued. "With the wedding ring. Hairy hands. We see you, hairy hands. And . . . we have you surrounded."

The hand didn't move, didn't even twitch. Amy had the sinking feeling that they'd found a dead body. Someone had died in Bedrooms and there was no way they could leave a dead body for morning shift. Basil would insist on removing it before the Consultant Team arrived. This night was never going to end.

"Look, we've called the police," Basil tried again. "You can come out now or the cops will drag you out. Do you want to be pepper-sprayed? And Tasered?"

All at once, Ruth Anne strode past him, approached the bed and raised one end, revealing a man splayed out facedown like a starfish. He burst into motion, scuttling away like a bug after its rock has been lifted. Stumbling to his feet, he immediately whacked his head on the edge of the raised bedframe. He had too much momentum to stop, but the collision knocked him off-balance; he wove his way across the Bright and Shining Path, caught a Sploog love seat at midthigh, and went flying over it, head over heels.

"You better run!" Matt shouted.

"No, do not run!" Basil yelled. "Stop!"

The man pushed himself off the floor and limped into an ocean of desks, heading for the shortcut in Storage Solutions. "I said stop!" Basil called again. "The doors are locked! We've got you on tape!"

The man dropped his hands to his sides. His shoulders slumped as if he'd been unplugged. Then he turned around. He was balding, with a five o'clock shadow that looked like purple sandpaper. "You got me," he said, in a whiny nasal voice. "I'm gotten, okay?"

His blue polo shirt stretched over his belly; there were dried white sweat stains in the armpits. His khakis looked shiny at the knees. One of his sneakers had duct tape wrapped around the toes.

"Stay there," Basil said. "Don't move."

"I'm not moving," the man said.

"Why'd you jump my girlfriend?" Matt snapped.

"I jumped her? No way, man. I bumped into her and got scared out of my socks. I tried to get away. If anything, *she* jumped *me*. I would never raise my hand against a woman. I'm a committed pacifist! I don't know what she told you guys."

"He didn't jump me," Trinity said. "He tried to communicate with me." She raced up to the man, pointing her camera at his face. "How long have you been dead?"

"He's not a fucking ghost," Matt snapped in frustration. "He's just homeless. He's a bum. Don't get too close."

"You don't have to call me names," the guy said, looking genuinely crestfallen. Then he turned to Trinity. "But your boyfriend's right, sweetheart. I'm no ghost."

"He's not my boyfriend," Trinity said. "And I know you aren't a ghost. Ghosts don't hide under beds."

Then she sat down on a Scopperloit chair and began to cry.

"Oh, honey," Ruth Anne said, rushing to her.

"I'm fine," Trinity said with a sob. "Really, I'm fine."

"Who are you?" Basil demanded. "You can't be in here."

"I'm Carl," the man said.

"Carl who?"

"I would prefer not to say."

"Do you have any ID?"

"Are you busting me?" Carl asked.

"I'm not busting you," Basil said, making air quotes around the word *busting*. "But I am responsible for this store. How did you get inside?"

"Same way I do every night," Carl said. "I hang out in the café until closing, then I go to the bathroom around nine thirty and sit in the stall and pull my feet up on the commode whenever the door opens. Your security guys do a terrible job, by the way. You should find a new company."

Trinity was still sobbing as though she might never stop, and Ruth Anne was gently rubbing her back. Matt stood off to one side, looking awkward.

Basil turned to Amy. "This is the guy you saw?"

"I was pretty far away," she said. "But I think so."

"Oh!" Carl exclaimed, as if Amy had just cleared up something that was bothering him. "You're the gal from this morning. I hope I didn't scare you. I thought for sure you would call security."

"Did you vandalize a Brooka?" Basil asked.

"A what?"

"A Brooka sofa. When we opened the store this morning, one of the sofas was . . . soiled. With a substance."

"Poop," Amy added.

Carl blushed. "Look," he said to Basil. "Can I talk to you privately? Man to man?"

Basil made an "I got this" gesture to his team. "Stay here. I'll be right back," he said, and then he took Carl by the arm and steered him a few steps down the Bright and Shining Path.

"Here's the thing," Carl explained. "I haven't been well lately. I don't totally know what happened last night."

"Are you on drugs?"

Carl looked distressed. "I get these headaches. I got epilepsy, did I tell you that? Sometimes I black out. And when I wake up, I got dirt on me or glass in my hair. Look at my hands." He held them out. His fingernails were black. "They were clean when I went to bed last night."

"You don't remember anything?" Basil asked.

"I had pills. But I can't get my prescription filled no more."

"How long have you been sneaking in here?"

"Please don't get angry. It's just a place for me to sleep. And use the john. I've never stolen a thing."

"But you're breaking stuff," Basil said. "Mirrors, curtains, glassware—"

"No, never, I swear," Carl insisted. "I've treated this place like I would treat my own home. That's your motto, isn't it? A Home for the Everyone? This is *my* home."

"No, this is a place of business."

"I got nowhere else to go," Carl said. "I tried hiding out in Lowe's and Ikea but they've got much better security. Can't you guys show a little sympathy?"

He directed this last comment over Basil's shoulder to Amy, Ruth Anne, Matt, and Trinity, who were all standing right behind Basil.

"My wife's got my little girl," Carl continued, "and I can't visit with her until I've got some kind of place to live that's not a shelter bed. So I took the bus out here to fill out a job application and I was walking around thinking, This place is way better than the shelter, you know? And so I sort of stuck around. You got great prices in the café."

"You're a victim of the economy," Basil said, offering something.

"You can say that again," Carl agreed.

Amy saw Basil get a shifty, thoughtful look, and she knew he had found his teachable moment. After spending most of the night trying to establish his authority, he was finally going to close the deal.

"I'm afraid this isn't my decision to make," Basil

said. "Here at Orsk, we're a team. And as a team, we make our decisions together. That's called Orsk-Mindedness."

"It is?" Amy asked.

Basil went on. "Either we can let Carl walk out of here or we can call the police, but we will all vote and make the decision together."

"No police," Carl said. "Please."

"I'll vote first," Basil said, "and I vote police."

"Me, too," Matt said. "He could have hurt Trinity."

"I didn't hurt anyone," Carl protested. "Look, take me downstairs, snap a photo of me, and post it on your wall of shoplifters, so I can't ever come back here again. Then kick me out the front door like a dog. It's punishment enough to have to get back to Cleveland in the middle of the night; the shelters won't be open, but I'll go right now and I won't ever come back. Please, guys, I can't afford to get arrested. It'll just be more ammunition for my wife to take to the judge. You know, it's a war on fathers out there."

"I vote to let him go," Ruth Anne said. "The poor man has had enough hardship in his life."

"Thank you, ma'am," Carl said, sticking out his hand. "Pleased to meetcha. Thank you."

"Yeah," Trinity said. She had finally stopped sobbing. "I don't care. Whatever. Let him go."

Now they all turned to Amy. It was a tied vote, two to two. Like Ruth Anne, Amy didn't see the point in further punishing the guy. He was caught, and everything had a rational explanation. Maybe now Basil would call off the search and let them go home early.

"We should let him go," she said. "We're going to call the cops because of what? He didn't want to sleep in his car? I don't want to sleep in my car."

"I don't have a car," Carl said.

"All he did was break some stuff," Amy continued, ignoring him. "It's not even our stuff. Orsk can afford to replace it. Look, you got the guy messing with the store. Let's clean up and call it a night. Let him go."

"Fine," Basil said, irritated.

"Did I win?" Carl asked.

"You won," Amy said.

"Yes!" Carl shouted. "Thank you!"

He ran to Trinity and wrapped his arms around her, lifting her up in a bear hug. The mood shifted radically. Maybe it was relief after all the tension, but everyone except Basil was suddenly possessed by a spirit of giddy euphoria.

"There's one tiny problem," Ruth Anne said. "Amy already called the police."

"What?" Basil said. "Why? I specifically told you not to do that."

"I panicked," Amy said.

"Call them back," Carl said. "Tell them not to come."

"That's not how it works," Ruth Anne said, shaking her head. "You see it on *Cops* all the time. Once they get the call, they have to show up."

"I'm sorry," Amy said.

Basil cast an annoyed glance in her direction. "I'll fix this. Here's what we're going to do. I'll go downstairs and stand outside. I'll wait for the police and I'll complete the necessary paperwork, tell them it's a false alarm. Once the coast is clear, we'll kick Carl out of here. Seem fair?"

"Whatever you say," Carl said, pumping Basil's hand. "I owe you everything. Thank you for being a good guy. Thank you!"

Basil managed to extract his hand. "Everybody stay here until I get back."

"Again, thank you," Carl repeated.

"Enough already," Basil said, and he set off toward the front of the store.

Carl went around shaking hands with everyone, introducing himself and learning their names. "I really appreciate your vote," he told Amy. "It's a good thing you've done for me tonight. You're good people. I won't forget it."

"Uh, thanks?" Amy said, embarrassed.

An awkward silence ensued. Dining Rooms wasn't the best place to kill time, and they all acknowledged the moment with forced smiles.

"Did anyone bring cards?" Ruth Anne joked.

"This whole night is ruined," Trinity said.

A tinny snatch of music played from Amy's pocket. She pulled out her cell phone and answered it. "Hello?"

"This is the Brecksville Police Department dispatcher. Did you call 911?"

"Yes, but—"

"And your address is 7414 River Park Drive?"

"It is, but we don't need—"

"How do you get there?" the dispatcher asked.

"It depends which way you're coming," Amy said. "Don't you guys know this? You take any exit along Cuyahoga and you get on the feeder road. There's not an exit from the highway."

"So they have to get on the feeder road?" the dispatcher asked.

"Yeah," Amy said.

"I'll let them know. If we have any more problems,

can I reach you at this number?"

"Sure, but my battery's getting low," Amy said. "Also, you guys don't need to come because—"

The dispatcher hung up.

"The bad news is that the cops are still coming," Amy said. "The good news is that they're lost."

"This is turning into a long night," Ruth Anne said. She turned to Matt. "Did you two find any ghosts?"

"Not unless you count Carl," Trinity said.

Matt sat down heavily on one of the Scopperloit chairs.

"Tonight's been all teasing and no pleasing," he said. "Without a money shot, our reel is going to be all buildup and no payoff."

Carl noticed that Matt was carrying a video camera. "Wait, you guys are ghost hunters? Like on A&E?"

"Would everyone stop talking about A&E?" Matt said. "There *are* other channels."

"They want to be on Bravo," Amy explained to Carl.

"With the *Real Housewives*," Ruth Anne added helpfully.

"But ghosts only haunt houses," Carl said. "Everybody knows that."

"This is a building with bedrooms, bathrooms, kitchens, and dining rooms," Matt said. "If that's your definition of a house, then Orsk is a house. 'A Home for the Everyone.' People come here all day long just to hang out, eat meatballs, leave their kids in Playland, browse, have coffee. You said it yourself: this place was your home."

"I guess so," Carl said. "Huh. Yeah, when you put it like that. This place does get pretty spooky after hours. You could have a séance in here."

He laughed to himself but stopped when he noticed Trinity staring at him. Carl grew uncomfortable as Trinity kept staring. He shifted around a little, but she was boring into him with her eyes.

"What'd I say?" he asked. "I wasn't making fun of you or nothing. Honest."

"You're a genius," Trinity said. "You. Are. A. Genius!"

"I am?" Carl said.

"Matt," Trinity said. "Get the gear! We'll have a séance!"

"Viewers love séances," Matt said, warming up to the idea. "And they come across great on camera."

"We'll grab candles from Home Decorations," Trinity said. "And use the Frånjk for the table. The one with the black finish. It looks like the hood of a hearse."

"We'll have to hurry before Basil comes back," Matt said.

"I don't think that's happening anytime soon," Amy said. "But you still have one major problem. Isn't the store too bright for a séance?"

Matt looked down at his wristwatch and at that moment nearly all of the store's six hundred eighty fill lights clicked off at once, plunging the Showroom into a twilight gloom. A thousand shadows leapt from their hiding places. The furniture suddenly seemed strange, oversized, bigger than it ought to be. Ruth Anne let out a little yelp.

"Happens automatically," Matt said. "Every night at 2 a.m."

"Perfect timing," Trinity said, grinning at the others. "Now, who's in?"

FRÅNJK 08

Dining is not about the table and chairs. It's about the conversations and companions that you invite into your home, making memories that will sparkle tonight and last forever. **FRÅNJK** is the frame—your life is the picture.

AVAILABLE IN NIGHT BIRCH AND BEAVER OAK
W 92¾ X D 32¼ X H 34¼
ITEM NUMBER 6666434881

After they convinced Ruth Anne that
what they were doing was not "satanic" in any way,
shape, or form, the next big objection came from Amy.

"I don't want to hold hands," she said.

"Trust me," Matt said. "I have a way to complete
the circle without holding hands."

The final obstacle was convincing Carl to partic-
ipate. Matt explained that three participants would
not offer enough production value and that four people would look too symmetrical on camera. "The
best-looking séances always have five people," he said.
"It's five or nothing."

"It feels a little spooky," Carl said. "But I guess it'd
be rude not to."

With everyone on board and the clock ticking
against Basil's return, Matt and Trinity ran around
the Showroom like hyperactive puppies. The few
remaining fill lights afforded just enough illumina-
tion for them to find their way around. Matt hauled

over a couple of gear bags and set up the tripods and cameras. Trinity ran down to the Market Floor and galloped back with a box of vanilla-scented votive candles that she deployed around the dining room display. By the time she was finished, it looked like a romantic lovemaking scene in a made-for-TV movie.

"I can't believe I'm doing this," Amy said.

"Believe it," Matt said. He positioned the cameras around the Frånjk in a loose circle and then dropped an EMF reader in the center of the table.

"The *Ghost Bomb* audience is going to love this," Trinity said.

"But a séance doesn't actually summon anything, does it?" Ruth Anne asked.

"Sure it does," Trinity said.

"No, it doesn't," Amy said.

"We'll have a great reel no matter what," Matt said. "There's no way to screw up footage of a séance."

Once they were finished setting up, Trinity directed everyone to their seats. Carl took the end of the table, with Trinity on his left and Ruth Anne on his right. Matt sat beside Trinity, across from Amy.

"And now," Matt said, digging into his bag. "I told you there'd be no unsanitary hand-holding."

He pulled out his solution with a flourish.

"Oh, no, Matt," Ruth Anne said. "No way. Uh-uh."

"Are you kidding?" Amy asked.

Like a magician fanning out a deck of cards, Matt revealed five pairs of silver handcuffs and flashed an evil grin.

"It ensures that no one breaks the circle," Trinity said. "And that no one reaches under the table and fakes spirit activity."

"And it looks *amazing* on camera," Matt said.

Carl shrugged. "Your house, your rules," he said, and then reached for a pair of cuffs. He placed one of the bracelets over his left wrist, and the hasp slid into the ratchet with a *click-click-click-CLICK.*

"You rock!" Trinity said.

"I want to see the key," Amy insisted.

Matt patted the pocket of his hoodie. "Right here."

"I want to test it."

Matt retrieved the key and spun it across the table-top. Amy inserted it into her cuffs, confirming that it really worked and she wouldn't be handcuffed inside an Orsk for the rest of the night. Then she leaned across the table and placed the key in the center.

"It stays right there," she insisted. "I don't want to have one of those stupid sitcom moments where no one can find the key."

"You got it," Trinity said.

"Basil is going to kill us," Amy said, but she click-click-clicked the cuffs around her left wrist and offered the other end to Ruth Anne.

"Last time I wore handcuffs was 1988," Ruth Anne said. "Spring Break in Myrtle Beach, South Carolina."

"Story, please!" Trinity said.

"A bunch of us got in a fight with a couple of Hells Angels," Ruth Anne said. "We lost, but I got in my licks. When we finally got out of jail the next night, they bought us a case of beer and we partied on the beach until sunup."

"You are a remarkable woman," Carl said.

"Did you get that on tape?" Trinity asked Matt.

Ruth Anne blushed, allowed herself one final application of Blistex, and then snapped the cuffs shut around her right wrist, securing herself to Amy. "Feels like old times," she said.

Matt and Trinity fussed over their equipment right until the last second, checking the viewfinders to make sure their shots were lined up and running around with Trinity's Zippo lighting all the candles. Finally, Trinity sat down and handcuffed herself to Carl; Matt flitted from one camera to the other, pressed Record on each of them, and slid into the chair next to Trinity.

"The final trick," he said, slipping Amy's extended handcuff over his left wrist and snapping it shut. Because they were sitting across from each other, he and Amy had to stretch their arms across the table-top. Then Matt stood his other cuff on the table, set his wrist into it, and used his beard to snap it shut. "Voilà!"

The circle was complete. Trinity raised her wrists and rattled them.

"We are locked down!" she said. "Everybody comfy?"

"I have to pee," Amy said.

"Shut up," Matt said.

"You're *sure* this isn't satanic?" Ruth Anne asked.

"It's a nondenominational séance," Trinity said.

"Just for pretend," Matt said to Ruth Anne. "Like a Ouija board."

"Now," Trinity said, speaking over him, "we sit silently until I ask the spirits to talk to us. I guess? I don't know. I've never done this before. Let's just be quiet for a minute."

No one said anything. There was the occasional scrape of handcuffs against wood and the jingle of chains as people adjusted themselves. Amy wanted to scratch her right side, but there wasn't enough slack for her to reach from her left to her right without pulling Ruth Anne out of her chair. Slowly the handcuff noises settled, and then they all began listening to the great silent store.

Someone's stomach rumbled and Amy tried hard not to laugh. She looked up and saw Trinity stifling a giggle and that put her over the edge.

"Sorry," Carl said. "That's me."

"Get that man a meatball," Amy said, which made Trinity laugh even harder.

"Sh!" Matt said. "We don't have a lot of disc space."

They quieted down for a minute, and this time the silence lasted for almost fifteen seconds. Then an unearthly moan filled the dining room display.

"OOOoooooo . . . ."

Amy turned to Ruth Anne, who had her eyes closed.

"I want . . . to speak . . . to your manager . . . " Ruth Anne moaned.

They all burst out laughing again—all except Trinity.

"Come on," she said. "Basil will be back any minute. Get serious."

"Okay, okay," Ruth Anne said. "I'm sorry. I'll be good."

There were a few more giggles, moans, and strange noises, but eventually the group settled down. Trinity closed her eyes, and Ruth Anne and Carl followed her example, but Amy glanced around the room. The candles flickered in the gloom, throwing shifting light over the Orsk wall posters. "Our home is forever," read one. "A place for the everyone for always," read another. Matt caught Amy's eye and she glanced away, pointlessly embarrassed. She felt like she'd been caught with her eyes open during Thanksgiving grace.

The overpowering scent of the candles was starting to give Amy a headache. The enormity of the store stretched out around them, and the silence pressed down like pressure on the ocean floor.

"Spirits?" Trinity called.

Her voice shattered the silence, and Amy flinched.

"Are you there, spirits? Can you hear me?"

Ruth Anne stretched out her hand and patted Amy's wrist reassuringly.

"Spirits," Trinity repeated. "Are any of you present tonight? If you hear my voice, give us a sign."

There was no noise. Not a sound. Amy realized she was listening as if she expected an answer. They were all listening. The cloying chemical stink of vanilla seemed to be crowding all the oxygen out of the room.

"Spirits," Trinity continued. "We come in peace, to let you communicate with us and tell us what you want. We know that you were imprisoned here unfairly so long ago, and we want you to know that we wish to hear your stories. You were forbidden to speak then, but you're free to speak now. Speak, O spirits. Speak."

Trinity had never sounded so sincere, not in all the time Amy had known her. Trinity really, truly believed this stuff. And only then did it occur to Amy that this séance could in fact be dangerous. Who knows what they might be opening themselves up to? But it was too late. It had started and now it had to run its course.

There was nothing to do but listen. Amy closed her eyes and listened to the whirring of the cameras as their motorized lenses zoomed in and out, their irises adjusting automatically. Her hearing moved past them, past the shiftings and scrapings of the people around the table, past the clatter of handcuffs. She heard the bass roar of the massive HVAC system, and she listened past that. She heard the wide, unnatural emptiness of the store, then the gurgle of pipes in the walls. She heard the building creaking and popping as it settled around them. Then her hearing sailed outside the building and she imagined she could hear the crunch of Basil's sneakers in the parking lot as he paced in circles, waiting for the police.

And then another noise—much closer. A soft, wet sound. Someone breathing. It came from across the table. Amy's concentration snapped into focus, but it took some effort to swim up through her layers of awareness and finally open her eyes.

It was Trinity. Her eyes were closed, and in the mellow candlelight Amy thought she could see them flickering back and forth underneath their lids. Her mouth was hanging open, her fists were balled on the table, clenched hard inside their silver bracelets, and her nose was running. A thin trickle of snot collected on her upper lip until her heavy breathing sucked it into her open mouth. A dozen wisecracks sprang to mind, but Amy resisted the urge to say anything. Everyone was being so serious.

The snot kept flowing, more and more of it, streaming over Trinity's upper lip and trickling into her mouth. It was disgusting. Amy glanced over at Matt, but his eyes were closed. They all had their eyes closed. Amy shifted in her chair. Shouldn't someone say something? Or maybe wake Trinity up? She wouldn't want this in her *Ghost Bomb* reel.

Finally Trinity's mouth was full and the snot spilled out, stretching toward the tabletop, a thin silver strand of drool hanging from her lower lip. It began to stretch and descended, quivering toward the tabletop, swinging gently back and forth, until its pendulous head tapped the front of Trinity's T-shirt and stuck there.

Amy couldn't stand it anymore. "Hey," she whispered.

With a sudden wet gasp, Trinity opened her eyes and tried to swallow. Her throat flexed and she choked on the thick glutinous mass. She gagged and gagged again, unable to get it all down. She reached for her neck, but her handcuffed wrists couldn't get close enough.

"Matt!" Amy called.

"It's okay," Matt said to Trinity. "I'm here."

Ruth Anne opened her eyes. "What's happening?"

"She's choking. Get these cuffs off."

"It's okay," Matt repeated. "Just spit it up, Trin. Get it out."

Trinity's throat gave a final heave and what Amy saw next was impossible: it looked like she was vomiting underwater. A thick, milky liquid hung in front of Trinity's face, an impossible cloud suspended in midair, soft white tendrils unfurling in slow motion.

"Get her cuffs off," Amy repeated, but either Matt didn't hear her or he was too awestruck to respond.

More fluid surged from Trinity's mouth, thickening the milk cloud. Candlelight reflected on its undulating surface, amplifying every delicate tremor, making it appear alive. As Trinity regurgitated gulp after gulp of white fluid, its aimless drift took on a purpose, unrolling tendrils back toward her face, latching onto her hair, her ears, clinging to her cheeks and dragging itself over her, obliterating her features beneath its milky ripples. The cloud pulled itself slowly over Trinity's head, engulfing her from the shoulders up until all that was left was a torso disappearing into a white glob of liquid, its sides rippling with surface tension as if it was breathing for her.

Trinity's chest heaved and her diaphragm and stomach jerked as she pumped out more fluid; the liquid mass thickened and bulged. Some distant part of Amy's mind understood that the Brooka/bathroom smell had returned, a rich toilet stench, stale and rank like rotten cheese.

The only person not watching the ectoplasm was Carl. His eyes were closed and he was breathing heavily through his nose. His face was red, his neck was corded. Sweat had blackened the collar of his polo shirt.

A long pseudopod of milky white fluid stretched across the table toward Carl and sniffed the air around him. He opened his eyes just as the fluid rolled over his face in an intimate gesture and flowed up his nostrils. Amy wanted to gag but she couldn't speak, she couldn't move. She was paralyzed watching this foul communion. The fluid stretched across the table from Trinity's mouth to Carl's nose, rippling in midair over the table like fabric floating underwater.

"Heh . . . hel—" Carl mumbled.

The ribbon of fluid fluttered, shaken by the sound

of his voice. Then its tail broke free of Trinity's mouth, and quick as an eel it disappeared up Carl's nose. As suddenly as it had appeared, it was gone—and the spell that paralyzed the group was broken.

"Okay," Amy said, trying out her voice, relieved that she could speak. "Okay, okay."

"Is he—" Ruth Anne whispered.

"Hurts!" Carl said, loudly. "Forgot . . . it hurts!"

His voice was different; it was deeper and didn't sound like Carl at all. His hands spasmed and clenched in their cuffs, like dying crabs flexing on the table. A long minute passed before he spoke again, but when he finally did, he was considerably calmer. "Forgive me," he whispered. "Why does it always have to hurt so much?"

Trinity's head was lolling backward, as if her neck had been broken. Her eyes were closed. Her trance was still in effect. Her voice was a croak. "Who are you, spirit?"

Carl looked down at his wrists. All of his insecurity, all of his weakness, all of his kindness, all of it was gone. "You have me in restraints? That is too misguided. You are sicker in your spirits than I first believed."

"Who are you?" Trinity asked again.

"I am your warden, your healer. I am your north star. Your dispenser of health and goodness. You shall learn to love me, like all of the penitents in my Beehive."

Cold sweat trickled down Amy's spine. She thought back to the graffiti in the bathroom.

Carson Moore/Beehive
~~3 YR~~
~~4 YR~~
~~5 YR~~
~~6 YR~~
~~7 YR~~
FOREVER

"They called it my Beehive because it hummed with the sound of industry," Carl continued, his sweat-soaked face earnest. "My partners grew fat off the labor of my penitents, but I truly cared for them. I prescribed the toil that purified their souls."

"Enough," Matt said, reaching across the table for the handcuff key, dragging Trinity's limp arm behind him. But in the midst of all the confusion, the key had vanished.

"The sad young lover," Carl said. "Sick at heart, chasing after something he can never have. I fear the cure shall be difficult for you, my lad."

"What the fuck are you talking about?" Matt blustered.

"I'll have you turn the crank," Carl said. "It shall cauterize your sense of romantic folly. One thousand and one, one thousand and two, one thousand and three, one thousand and four . . ."

"Where's the key?" Matt said, looking around the table. "Who has the key?"

"Ten thousand turns of the crank every day," Carl

continued. "Ten thousand today, ten thousand tomorrow, ten thousand the next day after that. There is no exit until you're cured, because the door of the Beehive only swings one way."

He turned away from Matt to study the rest of the group. "Did any of you think you were here by accident? I've been watching you for so long, picking the sickest from amongst your ranks and nudging the hand of fate to guide you into my care. Providence must smile upon me, because here you all are."

Amy wanted to say "Whatever." Something flip. Something to undermine him. To undercut his bullying. To show him that he couldn't talk to her this way. But she felt hollow and two-dimensional and useless.

"There's the spinster," Carl said, looking at Ruth Anne. "Still afraid of her Creepy Crawlies, still possessing the mind of a child. Her cure will be quite painful, I'm afraid, but pain is a sure sign of its efficacy."

Ruth Anne recoiled, and next Carl turned to Trinity.

"This one must be turned from her tempting ways," he said. "There is a treatment involving the crushing of one's body on the tread wheel that is most effective with fallen women."

Then he turned to Amy. She looked down at her lap, avoiding eye contact. She didn't want to be seen by him. She squirmed like a bug on a needle while his eyes stripped her of her clothes, stripped her of her skin, laid her open and revealed her workings on the dissecting table.

"And you," he smiled. "I've been looking forward to treating you most of all. I shall present you with a variation of my tranquilizing chair that will guide you to the fulfillment of your true nature. For this is not a penitentiary, you see. It is a mill. A mill to manufacture sound minds. It is quite easy to begin. Something I learned from the Serbian tribes. Churches are built where saints were martyred. A bridge requires a child in its foundations if it is to hold. All great works must begin with a sacrifice."

And with that, Carl stood. Ruth Anne jumped, expecting to feel her left arm pull away from the table, but empty handcuffs dangled from both of Carl's wrists. Somehow he had detached himself from her and Trinity without anyone noticing.

"Give me the key," Matt said, trying to sound brave.

Carl turned his burning gaze on him.

"My whip shall split your bestial hides and drive you on to work, for work is the moral treatment that will mend your degraded minds," he warned, his voice rolling like thunder across the Showroom floor. It was the voice of a preacher, a voice of the past, a voice for cathedrals, a voice from a time before microphones. It was a voice that denounced witches and flogged sinners. It was a voice that sang Latin while women burned at the stake and men were crushed beneath stones. "Now, let us make the necessary sacrifice for my great work to begin again. Let us use the materials at hand to fling wide the gates and open the door. Come inside my mill," he said, licking colorless lips with his pale tongue. "Come inside, and let hard work cure the weakness inside your minds."

With that, Carl took the empty cuff dangling from his left wrist and, holding it like a scythe, pressed the sharp end of the hasp against his windpipe. At first it looked as though he was scratching an itch—but then he forced the tip into his neck, pushing the handcuff's teeth into his throat. Ruth Anne shrieked. Amy couldn't look away. Carl pushed the hasp deeper into his neck, hooking it behind his trachea. Then he yanked on the chain. There was a wet crunching sound, and a bib of black blood cascaded down him.

Matt stepped backward and tipped his chair over, pulling Trinity's limp body with him. She flopped to the floor, pulling him down in a kind of grim slapstick. Their fall jerked Amy across the table. The edge of the Frånjk caught her in the stomach and she let out a soft shocked grunt. The vanilla candles went rolling, spilling rivulets of white wax. Ruth Anne vaulted from her seat, but she was still tethered to Amy; the resistance yanked her back and she toppled a tripod.

Carl wavered where he stood, blood pulsing down his front. Then he slowly sat in his chair, face numb and glazed, mouth slack.

"Is he dead?" Matt asked. "Did he kill himself? Did we just watch this guy kill himself?"

"Stop pulling," Ruth Anne said to Amy, crawling onto the table, kicking candles out of her way.

"What?"

"Stay still."

Ruth Anne leaned over Carl's body, reaching into the pocket of his polo shirt. She retrieved the handcuff key from his pocket and unlocked her right wrist. She pulled her blouse over her head, slid off the table, put one hand behind Carl's head, and pressed her blouse to the gaping wound on his neck. Instantly, it was soaked in blood.

"Help me," she snapped at Amy, throwing her the key. "Get his legs."

Amy fumbled the key into her cuffs and released them. With one sweep of her arm, Ruth Anne cleared the table, sending the remaining candles and EMF reader clattering to the floor. Then she and Amy hoisted Carl's body onto the Frånjk. Ruth Anne kept her blouse pressed to his neck, applying pressure; she grabbed Carl's wrist and checked his pulse.

"Shit," she hissed, and let his wrist drop. Amy had never heard Ruth Anne curse before, and she knew it could mean only one thing.

"We shouldn't have done this," Amy said. "I knew it was a bad idea."

Ruth Anne lifted her blouse from the wound and spread it over Carl's face. Amy unlocked the others, and Matt helped Trinity to her feet. Her legs were wobbly and he had to hold her up.

"What happened?" she said, her voice hoarse. "I don't understand. Is Carl hurt?"

"What the hell is going on?" Basil asked.

He was standing in the center of the Bright and Shining Path, mouth hanging open, looking at a scene from his worst nightmare. Vanilla-scented candles had splashed wax halfway up the walls. Cameras were tipped over. Handcuffs were all over the floor. Ruth Anne was topless except for her bra. Blood was everywhere. And a dead man lay sprawled on a Frånjk dining table.

"Somebody answer me!" Basil said. "Who did this to him?"

"He did it to himself," Matt said. "He went crazy and tried to kill himself."

"It wasn't Carl," Amy said. "It was someone else. He said he was our warden. He said this place was his mill."

Trinity turned to her, awestruck.

"The séance worked?" she asked.

"What are you people talking about?" Basil said.

"You have to call the police," Amy said. "Call them and tell them to come back."

"They never showed up," Basil said, disgusted. "I came here to see if they called you back."

"I tried to save him," Ruth Anne said. "I really tried."

"Go clean up," Basil said. "There are T-shirts in the break room. And take Trinity with you. I don't want anyone alone. I'll come find you when the police get here."

"We found a ghost," Trinity said.

"Stop talking and go to the break room," Basil said. "I can't believe this is happening. There is a dead man on the Frånjk! And Corporate is going to be here in"— he looked at his watch—"five hours! We've got five hours to clean up and sort this out. This is a nightmare."

Trinity and Ruth Anne set off down the Bright and Shining Path.

Amy tried to explain. "It was nobody's fault," she said. "We were having a séance and—"

"A séance?" Basil asked. "Jesus Christ."

"It's true," Matt said. "He was possessed. Or something."

"Stop talking," Basil said. "Both of you. Stop talking."

He pushed past them and walked over to the Frånjk. Carl's face was still covered with the blouse. Basil tried to lift it, but the blood was already drying;

it came loose with a ripping sound.

Amy had seen two dead bodies before. The first was her uncle who had died, as they say, peacefully in his sleep. The other was a neighbor who'd overdosed at the trailer park. Carl looked worse than either of them. His eyes bulged like boiled eggs, his mouth was drawn down in a rictus of pain, and she couldn't even look at his throat. Amy felt Basil slump, defeated.

"We should . . . " she said.

"Not yet," Basil said, and he sounded exhausted. "Just give me a minute before you start talking."

Carl's hand shot out and seized Amy's wrist. Amy let out a yelp of surprise. His eyes rolled down and fixed on her. His mouth twisted itself into a cold grin. When he spoke, his voice seemed to creep out of the wound in his throat:

"The doors are open."

MESONXIC 09

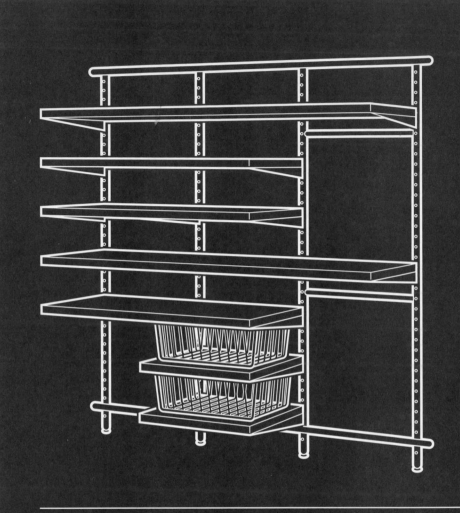

You need a closet that works for you, not the other way around. Our **MESONXIC** system is the foundation of your day, creating order out of chaos. Let it take care of your clothes while you take care of yourself.

Amy heard a distant click and her vision went black. The spotlights went dark. The exit signs. Power indicator lights. Everything. With no windows or skylights, the Showroom was blacker than midnight, and Amy was blind, isolated from everyone else, lost in darkness. She stumbled backward and at some point realized that Carl had released her wrist.

"The safety lights," a disembodied voice said.

Amy recognized the voice. Basil was somewhere to her left.

"No one can turn off the safety lights," he continued. "This is impossible."

The Showroom floor was massive, but Amy felt the walls and ceiling closing in. Her pulse was popping in her wrists, throbbing in her neck like a headache. But it wasn't the darkness that frightened her. It was the silence.

Normally she could hear the endless roar of Orsk's air-conditioning system blowing through the miles of ductwork, but now it was completely silent. The darkness was eating every sound, muffling it, muting it. The air felt warm and suddenly stale.

"Use your phones," Matt said.

Eerie blue light bloomed in the darkness as Matt powered on his iPhone and increased its screen brightness to the highest setting. Amy powered up her flip phone and realized that her battery was down to its last bar. She aimed the screen in Matt's direction and saw him squatting over a gear bag, rummaging inside. "It's got to be in here someplace," he said.

"The safety lights never go out," Basil repeated. "Not even in an earthquake."

This is worse than an earthquake, Amy thought. *This is something the Orsk engineers never anticipated.*

"Here." Matt switched on the Maglite and cast the beam around the dining room display. That's when they discovered that they were alone in the darkness. Except for a few spatters of blood and candle wax, the surface of the Frånjk was bare.

"What the hell?" Matt said.

"Oh, thank God," Basil sighed. "He's just injured."

"That's not possible," Amy said. "You didn't see what we saw."

Basil snatched the Maglite away from Matt and shone it around the Showroom floor, its beam bouncing across furniture and room displays, chasing away shadows. "Carl!" he called. "Can you hear me?"

Amy turned to Matt. "This is crazy. You saw what happened. We need to go."

If she had any courage, she would have walked out by herself, but the darkness was too complete. Her pathetic cell phone was too faint to guide the way. Amy had never been scared of the dark, or of ghosts, or of serial killers, but right now she felt small and vulnerable and surrounded by something hungry. Ruth Anne's talk of Creepy Crawlies echoed in her mind; they haunted the thick shadows, creeping closer and closer.

"Amy's right," Matt said. "We have to go."

"With an injured man bleeding all over the Showroom? I can't do that, Matt."

"He sliced open his throat," Matt said. "He killed himself."

"If he was dead, he'd still be on the table." Basil stepped out on the floor, aiming the flashlight toward Bedrooms. "Carl?"

Amy turned to Matt. "Please, let's get out of here. We're safer if we go together—"

"I have to get Trinity," Matt said. "I can't leave her in here."

"Fine. We'll go by the break area and get Trinity and Ruth Anne. Then we'll all leave together."

"Carl!" Basil shouted with relief. "Are you okay?"

Amy followed the beam of Basil's flashlight across the Bright and Shining Path to the Sylbian bedroom display. It was purple with white trim that made it look like an elderly woman's guest bedroom, and Amy had always imagined that it smelled like lavender. In the back left-hand corner was a doorway leading to a short hall fitted with the Mesonxic closet organization system. That's where Carl stood, staring at them.

"You really scared us," Basil said.

Amy could see the wound pulled across Carl's throat, his blood black in the flashlight beam. His eyes were bulging. One of his eyes had rolled up inside his skull so that only the white was showing, while the other stared sightlessly up and to the left. Still grinning, he stood completely motionless.

Then Carl raised one hand and beckoned them closer.

"Oh, crap," Amy said.

"We're getting out of here," Matt said.

Carl slipped sideways into the walk-in closet, disappearing from view. Basil started forward, taking the light with him. Matt grabbed his arm. "Amy's right," he said. "This is crazy. Let's leave this for the professionals."

"I *am* a professional," Basil said. "This is what being a professional means. You can't just walk away from a disaster and hope someone else cleans it up."

He went after Carl, and Matt and Amy followed. Staying in the darkness was not an option. If Basil had the light, they had to follow. They stepped into the Sylbian bedroom set and the maple floor creaked beneath their feet. They walked to the rear of the bedroom display, the air getting thicker with every step, and rounded the corner into the narrow closet.

The short hallway was designed to showcase the Mesonxic closet storage system—a series of shelves, cubbies, drawers, and hanging rods that made optimal use of even the smallest space. Three white dress shirts on display hangers swayed slightly in a cold breeze. At the end of the narrow purple hallway was another fake wooden door, like the one Amy had shown Ruth Anne earlier. A cheap optical illusion cut into drywall to fool the eye.

The door was ajar.

"I'm going to throw up," Amy said.

"Not on the stock," Basil said.

"It doesn't open," Amy said. "That door doesn't open. It *can't* open."

Basil pulled on the handle and the door swung open, revealing the entrance to a long dark hallway. Until he'd opened the door all the way, Amy could pretend that maybe this was just a mirage, a weird shadow, something to do with the EMF stuff Matt had been talking about. But this was no trick. This hallway couldn't be here. This hallway was impossible.

And if this door opened, what about the other fake doors? What about the fake windows? If she went around the store and lifted all the blinds, what would she see?

A cold wind, putrid and marshy, blew out of the doorway, ruffling Amy's hair. She felt like she was standing in front of an open refrigerator full of rotten food. The display shirts swung wildly on their hangers. It was the Brooka smell again, the bathroom smell, the smell of the séance.

"This is a hallucination," Amy said, desperately wanting to believe her own words. "You try to walk through that door and you'll break your nose."

The glow from the Maglite lit up the first few feet of the hall. Its white plaster walls were rank with yellow water stains. Its dirty floor was unfinished concrete. It stretched for twenty feet before taking a sharp turn to the right.

"Did you hear that?" Basil asked.

The three of them listened.

"I didn't hear anything," Matt said.

"It's Carl," Basil said. "He's in there."

Then he walked through the closet and stepped over the threshold, and the hallway swallowed him whole. Matt started to follow and Amy grabbed his arm.

"Don't," she said.

"He's got the light," Matt said. "We'll never find our way out in the dark."

"But this isn't the way out. This is the way *in*. It's all wrong."

"We have to stick together," Matt said.

He twisted out of her grip, followed Basil into the closet, and entered the impossible hallway.

Amy could see Matt and Basil, backlit by their flashlight, walking away from her down the corridor, and she hurried after them. At the end of the narrow Mesonxic she hesitated and then stepped into the doorway.

Immediately the tight walls shut her off from the store like a fist closing around her skull. Matt and Basil were a few steps ahead, the wall at the end of the hall getting brighter as they got closer, the shadow of the corner bouncing up and down.

Amy's feet crunched down the dirty hallway behind them. In the bright white circle of the light, the walls looked sick, covered in overlapping stains and mildew blooms. "We need to get out of here," she said to their backs, panic bubbling in her voice. She didn't want to be scared, but it was a physical body-wide reaction she couldn't fight. "Seriously, guys, the store doesn't go this way. This hall shouldn't be here. It shouldn't even exist. We should not be in here."

Something shocked Amy's leg and she jumped.

"Yah!"

Matt and Basil instantly whirled around.

"It's my phone," she said gratefully, pulling the vibrating cell out of her pocket with both hands and showing it to them. "Hello?"

"This is the dispatcher at the Brecksville Police Department. Our unit still can't find the feeder road. Are you sure it's off Route 77?"

"I drive here every day," Amy said. "Don't you have GPS or something?"

"The computer is showing that address you gave me is invalid," the dispatcher said.

"What does that mean?"

"It means that, according to our system, the address doesn't—"

The woman's voice cut off and the phone's screen went black. Amy pressed the Power button but her phone was dead, useless as a brick.

"What did they say?" Basil asked.

"I'm not sure they're coming," Amy said. "We might be on our own."

"I know you two are panicking," Basil said. "But we need to find Carl. He—"

"He's not Carl anymore," Amy said. "You weren't there. You didn't see what we saw. Trinity called out to all the spirits in the store. She invited them to join us. And something in the store took over Carl. He called himself a warden. A healer of souls. He said we were all penitents—"

"Josiah Worth!" Matt realized, turning to Amy. "That's the guy I was telling you about earlier. The warden of the Cuyahoga Panopticon. The prison from the nineteenth century."

"Oh, enough with the *Ghost Bomb* crap," Basil

said. "Carl is a homeless man in severe mental distress. Per the Orsk Leadership Culture Handbook, we need to find him, comfort him, and call for medical assistance. That's official store policy." He aimed his flashlight down the hall. "The guy's probably halfway to Bedrooms by now."

"This hall doesn't go to Bedrooms," Amy said. "It goes to the Beehive. To a nineteenth-century prison. Please stop acting like this hall is normal. You must know it doesn't really exist."

"Of course it exists," Basil said. "We're standing in it, aren't we?"

"It could be a hallucination," Matt said. "A product of EM fields or some kind of toxic venting."

"You really think so?" Basil asked.

Matt punched the wall as hard as he could. The impact shook loose a shower of damp plaster flakes. He unclenched his fist and shook out his hand.

"Nope," he said. "I guess not."

"Please, Basil," Amy said. "We have to turn around. I respect that you're a store manager and you've been trained for these situations, but I'm scared, okay? I'm your employee and I'm frightened, and I'm asking for your help. Can we please turn around? Can we please find Trinity and Ruth Anne and get out of here?"

Basil hesitated, weighing the choice. Amy knew from taking the Shop Responsible test that Orsk managers had a responsibility to both store guests and store partners.

But what if a manager had to choose one over the other? What was the priority? These were questions the test hadn't posed, and Basil was struggling.

"Tell you what," he decided. "Let me just look

around the corner. If I see Bedrooms, we'll keep going. If I don't, I promise we'll turn around."

"Sounds good," Matt said. "Go take a quick peek and we'll wait right here."

"Hurry," Amy said.

Basil headed for the corner, taking the light with him. Amy stood still and tried not to touch the filthy walls. She could taste the swampy stink coating the roof of her mouth, turning her saliva bitter and sending it trickling down the back of her throat.

"Are you still here?" she whispered.

For a single, terrifying moment, Matt didn't answer. Then he illuminated his face with the pale blue glow of his phone. "Still here."

Up ahead, Basil was pointing his flashlight around the corner. He hesitated, squinting into the darkness, playing the beam back and forth over something.

"Basil?" Matt whispered.

Amy heard it first.

It wasn't quite a noise but a displacement of air, a feeling of something big that filled the hall, something big that was coming up from the depths. It was the sound of far-off movement. It was the sound of something coming for them. Amy broke.

"Go!" she said, turning around and running blindly into the dark, barreling back out of the hallway, shoulders banging into walls. Matt was right behind her, holding out his cell phone, supplying just enough light for them to see the doorway at the end of the corridor. Amy was certain it was going to slam shut at any moment, trapping them in the Beehive for good.

Then all at once they were outside, back in the clean orderly world of Orsk, back in the narrow walk-in closet, surrounded by the Mesonxic organization system. They kept running. They didn't wait to see if Basil made it out. He was on his own. They barreled out of the closet and into the room display, hit the Bright and Shining Path at full speed, and didn't stop until they swerved off and collapsed behind an island counter in a Kitchens display. Matt buried the glow of his cell phone in the folds of his hoodie.

"Did you see them?" he whispered.

"See who?"

"In that hall. There were people."

Amy didn't know what she'd seen and what she hadn't. They crouched behind the island, ears straining for any movement in the dark.

"What's that noise?" Matt asked.

Amy listened. She heard a gentle crystal ringing. Matt aimed his phone behind them at a shelf of Glans water goblets, all quietly chiming against one another. Then she felt the rhythmic vibration in the floor.

"Something's coming," she said.

Matt's cell phone flashed white. Its screen shattered.

He lunged away from her, and shattered glass smashed to the floor all around them as something invisible swiped the shelves clear. Amy ducked and squeezed her eyes shut as a torrent of shards rained down. Then there was silence. After a moment, Amy looked up.

"Matt?" she whispered.

He didn't answer. She couldn't see a thing. The store was completely black. She didn't even know which way she was facing.

"Matt?" she whispered. "Please, tell me you're

here."

No answer. Had he abandoned her in the dark? Was he crawling toward the front entrance right this second? And could she really blame him? Together they'd ditched Basil, and now Matt had ditched her. They were all on their own.

Then she heard it: shallow breathing in the darkness. She lunged toward the sound and brushed Matt's shirt with her fingertips. "Are you all right?" She ran her fingers up his arm and felt cold wet fabric caked with sand and grit. His flesh was cold; his skin was stone. And as Amy realized this person wasn't Matt at all, he was already pushing his rough fingers inside her mouth and toppling her to the floor.

HÜGGA

10

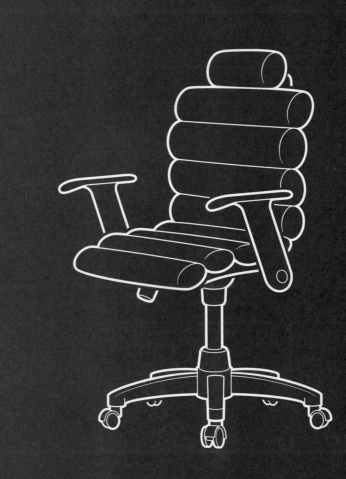

Introduce your home self to your work self with the adjustable rolling **HÜGGA**. Let the creativity you feel when you're at your most comfortable transform your workspace into a smartspace.

AVAILABLE IN NIGHT LEATHER
W 26¾ X D 32¼ X H 52¼
ITEM NUMBER 0666400917

Amy tried scrambling away but the hands found her and they were all over her, hundreds of hands, dragging her from her hiding place, pulling her across the floor, smashing her into walls and furniture. Twisting, screaming so loudly and for so long that she forgot she was screaming, Amy clawed at the maple flooring but only succeeded in peeling off one of her fingernails like a wet postage stamp. Cold, dirt-encrusted hands grabbed at her ankles, her wrists, her throat, her face. Amy's mind popped like a light bulb and only then did she finally go quiet.

After that it was all hands, dragging her, pushing and shoving and groping and pulling, and the whole time it was so dark she could have been asleep. Every breath she took was thick and filthy with the stench from the hallway.

People, or things that were shaped like people, thronged around her in a crushing mob, their muddy clothes suffocated her, the bodies underneath their rags as dead as marble; her head was filled with their stench, her bones were chilled by their cold. The hands lifted her up and slammed her down into a chair, knocking the wind out of her in one shocked gasp. Some distant part of her mind recognized it as a Poonang high-backed armchair with its cushion removed. A strap was cinched hard around her chest, and when she inhaled it tightened, collapsing her lungs, flattening her ribs, keeping her from drawing enough air to scream.

She tried to kick but the shapes in the darkness held her legs, and straps bit into her shins. The shapes forced her wrists down and fastened them to the arms of the chair, and then more bands encircled her flesh, more and more of them stretched over her thighs, around her knees, across her ankles, her waist, her shoulders, her neck. When she tried to move her head, she realized that it had been strapped to the back of the chair, leaving her no choice but to stare straight ahead.

Over the ripe stink, she smelled hot, scorched plastic and realized dimly that they were using the heat sealer, the one that locked thin plastic straps around bundles of cardboard in the trash room. Roughly, the hands tightened the straps, the sharp plastic edges slicing through her skin and muscle to grip bone.

All over her body, the bands cut into her flesh as they were pulled taut. She was a plastic bag full of blood being squeezed and compressed until she was about to burst. Breathing quickly and shallowly, she could barely deliver air to her lungs. A whine escaped her. It would have been a scream if she could have opened her mouth wide enough, but her jaw was strapped shut as well.

Where was she? Home Office? Bedrooms? It was too dark to know. Her surroundings were crowded with humanoid shapes, and she could feel the cold and the stink radiating from their bodies. Yet despite their presence, the space felt empty, as if everyone around her was hollow. As if they were un-persons. As if they weren't really there.

Then a voice whispered from the darkness.

"It's for your own good, you know."

Amy whimpered.

"Sh, sh, sh," Josiah hushed. "This is what you have always needed. You have no secrets from me."

Amy tried to struggle but was unable to move.

"I understand your madness," he whispered into her ear. Amy could hear the air wheezing in and out of the flap of torn skin across his throat. "Madness is an inflammation of your blood, an excitement of your arteries. My tranquilizing chair constricts the impetus of blood toward your brain and lessens muscular action, reducing the frequency of your pulse. If necessary, I may bleed you of inflammatory humors, or apply ice baths or boiling water treatments, without altering your position and without opposition."

Amy felt Josiah moving to the other side of her head. She strained to turn her eyes in his direction, trembling with effort as she tried to see him in the dark.

"Your madness is a typical case," Josiah said. "Your spirit is agitated and restless, and you engage in pointless activity, roaming about in an excitable frenzy to no great effect."

His words resonated with something deep inside

Amy's mind. She *did* run around, trying desperately to get somewhere, and what was the point? *Was* there a point?

"You want to be well," Josiah said. "That is the natural state for even a broken woman such as yourself. But although your spirit is willing, your flesh is weak. My tranquilizing chair allows you to stop fighting your nature. It masters your flesh. You will sit in contemplation here as your hot blood ceases its fevered circulation. And your brain, deprived of this poison, will at last achieve the stillness you crave. It is humane and merciful, a freedom from your torments. And if you die, isn't the stillness of death preferable to the vain agitation and senseless chaos of your life? It will be a great peace for you, Amy. A great peace."

A hand stroked the top of her head, and though she tried to recoil from its touch, she was unable to move. Eventually Josiah's hand stopped stroking her head, and then she didn't hear him anymore.

After a while, she didn't feel like Amy anymore.

She was a thing. A thing tied to a chair. And slowly she began to go insane.

She wasn't used to being completely still. In real life, Amy was always adjusting herself, moving, flexing, bending, unbending, rearranging her arms and legs. These options had been taken from her. She could feel her muscles cramping, her joints stiffening, the blood pooling in her swollen feet, and the frustration and pain made her want to scream. If only she could get enough air into her flattened lungs, or open her mouth wide enough to make a sound.

Her spine was pressed hard into the wooden back of the chair, becoming a column of pain running from her tailbone to the base of her skull. Her shoulders were on fire. Her neck burned from holding up her heavy skull. Her kneecaps ached as if they were going to tear through her skin. She felt everything below her knees go numb. But her fingers were the worst.

She tried to flex them, to wiggle each one just a tiny bit, but they were tied down so tightly it was as though something had closed its mouth around them and wouldn't let go. When she tried to stretch them, they only strained hopelessly against the bands. She felt gravity pulling blood into her fingertips, causing them to swell like juicy red grapes. With every heartbeat, she felt her pulse throb beneath her nails.

She was facing nothing, looking at nothing, surrounded by a darkness so profound she couldn't tell if her eyes were open or closed. With no input, set adrift inside her own skull, Amy's mind began to turn on itself. It began to sort through her twenty-four years and calculate what she had to show for all the fighting, all the struggle, all the scrimping, and saving, and double shifts, and finishing papers, and working on her portfolio. All that effort, all that pain—for what?

Every morning she woke up more exhausted than the morning before, every month her rent was late, every week she mooched groceries from her roommates. She never had enough gas, she was always borrowing money, she was constantly in debt, and still it wasn't enough. The hamster wheel kept turning faster and faster.

In a way, the chair was her friend. It freed her from all the illusions. It showed her the truth. She was alone. No one was there to help her. All her life she had run from the one thing she'd been born to do: wear a uniform and work a register. It was time to embrace her true nature.

The problem was the liars. They said she could do anything she set her mind to, they told her she should shoot for the moon because if she missed she'd be among the stars, they made movies tricking her into thinking she could achieve heroic things. All lies. Because she was born to answer phones in call centers, to carry bags to customers' cars, to punch a clock, to measure her life in smoke breaks. To think otherwise was insane. The chair didn't lie to her. The chair cured her of madness. The chair showed her exactly what she was capable of, and that was *nothing*.

Something floated up from the darkness inside Amy's brain, and she realized that she finally had her sit-down job. It was funny because it was true. This was the last thing she would ever do, and it was about time. She had failed and failed and failed, all the way from the beginning. She had failed to escape her mom's trailer, she had failed to earn her degree, she had failed the Shop Responsible test, she had failed to do anything with her life. That was her nature. Fail and quit. If you cut her open, it was fail and quit right down to her bones.

For years, Amy had wondered what would happen if she stopped fighting and let go. For as long as she remembered, she had been scared of how far she would fall if she stopped struggling. It was a relief to finally have an answer. *This far*. This was how far she would fall. This was the bottom.

A sense of relief numbed the pain as her limbs lost circulation. She could feel her mind getting better; she could feel it healing, sloughing off decades of lies and madness, accepting her place in the natural order. She would stay in this chair not moving, not doing anything, and there would be no more illusions, no more lies, no more useless struggle, no more failed attempts to escape. She was thankful for the chair. It was where she belonged.

Chest hitching, the bands around it so tight they kept her from drawing a breath, Amy became lightheaded. She could not move. She could not see. She could not hear. She could not breathe. And her only thought was a single loop running over, and over, and over again.

"I'm home . . . I'm home . . . I'm home . . ."

BODAVEST

11

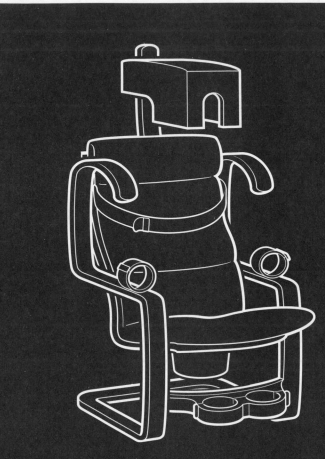

Boasting several advantages over traditional forms of restraint, **BODAVEST** confines the penitent and opposes the agitated movement of blood toward the brain, forcing the subject into a state of total immobility, conducive to self-reflection and free of stressful outside stimuli.

AVAILABLE IN LIGHT OAK AND MEDIUM BIRCH
W 24¾ X D 21¼ X H 53¼
ITEM NUMBER 5355666200

Hands. There were hands on her face like two soft spiders crawling over her skin. She couldn't gulp enough air to make a sound. All that came out was a pathetic mewling. The big sound, the insane sound, was still trapped inside her head.

Light smashed into her eyes. Her pupils contracted to pinpricks.

"Shhh, shhh, shhh. It's me, it's Basil. Are you okay?"

Amy wanted to turn her head away, but the straps held it in place. Because her eyes had grown accustomed to the darkness, she was blinded by the dim glow of his cell phone. If she'd been capable of speech, she would have told him to go away, to leave her alone. Basil ran his fingers over the straps, which were as taut and rigid as steel. Amy's body was numb. Circulation to her extremities had all but ceased; her limbs were as cold and lifeless as wood. Blood starved, they had floated away on a sea of pain, one by one.

Then Basil simply turned and walked away, taking his light with him. Amy closed her eyes and felt tears slipping down her cheeks. They were tears of relief. Now she could be alone again in the dark. It was cruel to make her think that someone had come for her. It was sadistic to make her think she was not alone when she knew that she was always alone. It was—

The strap holding her chin in place got tighter and tighter and then snapped and was gone.

She involuntarily sucked in a great mouthful of air—"Heeeeeeee!"—and gagged on it. Her lungs wouldn't inflate enough to force it all down.

"Take it easy," Basil whispered. "Small breaths."

He was crouched behind her chair, foolishly trying to rescue her from what she had already embraced. Taking away what she truly wanted just when she had finally found it. Pretending that she could get out of her chair. Telling her lies.

"A good manager carries a pocket blade at all times," he was saying. "You never know when a customer will need help opening a flat pack."

With a sudden snap, the straps binding her chest came loose. The instant rush of oxygen made Amy's head spin. She tried to talk but managed only nonsensical sounds. She could feel Basil working all around her, on her sides, behind her, slashing away with his knife. One by one, the straps on her fingers and wrists and forearms and elbows went slack. Each time there was a blessed moment of numbness, and then the limb exploded into fire as the blood rushed back, hammering pins and needles into the tips of her fingers and toes. It hurt so badly and what was the point? She wasn't going anywhere. Why couldn't he stop trying and leave her alone?

"Amy, please, talk to me," Basil said from the darkness.

Amy held very still, her body wracked with tremors.

"I've been stumbling around in the dark looking for anyone," he said. "All the power is out. The exit signs aren't working, the air is shut off, and, to be honest, if this is what that sick freak did to you, then I don't want to hang around and wait for him to come back. Come on."

Amy didn't move, she didn't speak. All she did was close her eyes and sink back into the darkness.

"I'm going to help you stand," Basil said.

She didn't talk. She hoped that if she didn't talk, he would go away.

Instead he stood behind her, grabbed underneath her armpits, and hauled her up. As her weight shifted, she felt boiling oil draining into her ankles and feet. The feeling was so excruciating that she slithered out of Basil's grip and slumped to the floor. Instinctively, she drew her legs into a fetal position, sobbing as she hugged her knees to her chest. She wanted to get back into her chair. It was so much *easier* in the chair.

Basil hooked a hand around her belt, braced his legs, and pulled her to a sitting position. She collapsed bonelessly against the wall.

"Go," she whispered. "Leave."

He squatted next to her, brushed her sweaty hair away from her face, and shined his cell phone into her eyes. They were unfocused, unseeing.

"I can't leave you here. I'm your supervisor. It's my responsibility to keep you safe."

Amy slumped over onto one side and tried to crawl

away. Her arms were on fire, her muscles felt like they'd been torn apart and stapled back together. They pulled and knotted in all the wrong directions, and they didn't fit inside her skin. Her body felt old and frail. Basil tried to stop her, but she kept crawling. She wanted to slither back into the darkness, she wanted this useless struggle to end. She mindlessly began to crawl along the wall.

Basil doesn't understand, Amy thought, *but if he keeps talking they are going to hear him, and they are going to come, and they are going to fix his sickness, too.* That thought made Amy smile.

"Don't worry," she said. "He'll make you whole again."

"Who will?"

"Warden Worth," Amy said.

"Do you mean Carl? The homeless guy? Is he Warden Worth?"

She tried to shake her head, but even this simple gesture triggered another excruciating flash of pain. "The warden is inside Carl. He wears Carl like a glove. The warden wants to help us."

"Amy, I don't know what you're talking about," Basil said. "But something's really wrong with you. Do you know where we are? What day it is?"

"We're in the Beehive," Amy said.

"There is no beehive. You're not thinking straight."

"It's where we get what we deserve."

"We're in Orsk," Basil said.

"No," she said. "We've always been in the Beehive. There is nowhere else."

"Right," Basil said. Again he tried lifting her, and again Amy went limp in his arms. When he paused to adjust his grip, she spilled back onto the floor. Basil walked away again, and this time she hoped he was gone for good. Amy let the blackness wash over her and carry her away. True, she no longer had the security of the tranquilizing chair, but as long as she didn't move or fight, as long as she surrendered, she could feel like she still was part of the Beehive.

There was a low rumble in the distance and Amy knew Warden Worth was coming back for her. He would return her to the chair, or perhaps he would administer a stronger cure. The rumble grew louder and Amy relaxed her body to welcome him. She was tired of feeling sick and broken. She wanted to be whole. She searched the darkness, waiting for her master.

Instead Basil's face emerged from the gloom, faintly illuminated by his cell phone. He was pushing a rolling Hügga office chair. As soon as he stopped moving, the rumbling stopped. He knelt beside her and said, "We're getting out of here."

"You can't comprehend his plans for us."

"You're right, Amy," he said. "I don't know what's going on. But I am still responsible for your safety."

He hauled her up by her arms, dumping her limp body into the Hügga. Amy tried to slide out but Basil was too quick. He grabbed her shoulders, holding her in place. With a gentle push he rolled the chair forward, and they set off down the Bright and Shining Path. The chair made an enormous racket, and Amy felt safe in the knowledge that all this noise would guide Warden Worth to them. She relaxed and looked around. A limp banner drooled from the ceiling. Most days it read "Bring new life into your home," but in the darkness she could make out only the last two words: *your home.*

Basil swung his cell phone back and forth, its dim gray glow enough to illuminate couches and arm-chairs but not strong enough to reveal whatever was crouched behind them. "Almost there," he said. "We'll get outside, and if we're lucky the police will be here. They'll help me get everyone else out."

"We're not going anywhere," Amy said.

Ahead of them, the Bright and Shining Path was blocked by a tall barricade of toppled furniture—a huge heaping mound of Ficaro storage units, Neli-pot media organizers, Gutevol rocking chairs, and smashed Kummerspeck desks. An overturned impulse bin was slung onto its side, beige shopping bags ava-lanching onto the floor. Broken glass was everywhere.

Amy remembered the filthy hands, slick with grime, sliding over her face. She wanted to run away but she needed to go back. Run away, or go back?

"We have to go the other way," Basil whispered.

He spun around to face Kitchens, and Amy smiled to herself. The more he struggled, the sooner he'd realize the hopelessness of their situation. They were never getting out. Warden Worth would just extend their sentences, adding years and years and years. He would be so angry that Amy had gotten out of her chair. He would be so angry she'd stopped her treatment.

Basil pushed her off the Path toward the shortcut door between Kitchens and Wardrobes, only to dis-cover it was barricaded with more smashed furniture. Alone, Basil might have climbed over it, but with Amy it was impossible.

"Not a problem," he insisted. "We'll take the long

way around."

He turned the chair back toward Dining Rooms. Amy realized that her lungs no longer hurt as badly. She was breathing more normally. Her head felt clearer, and the time spent in the restraining chair was receding from memory.

"You're trapped," she whispered.

"We're fine," Basil assured her, but his voice was a little less certain. "We'll simply have to go through the back of house."

One of the wheels on the Hügga began to squeak, making a steady *eek-eek-eek* as they rolled along, a clear beacon to anything waiting in the dark.

"There's nowhere to go," Amy said.

"We have to do something," Basil said. "We can't just crawl under a sofa and hide until the sun comes up."

The first thing that hit them was the cold—a blast of frigid air that snatched the breath from their throats. Then came the stink, so strong it made Amy's eyes water. It was like a train of rotten meat passing in the dark. It was so close and so enormous, it chased all thought of being cured from Amy's brain and left just one thing in its place: fear. Basil stopped rolling the chair and listened. Then he leaned down.

"Can you run?" he whispered into her ear.

Amy was too scared to answer. Of course she couldn't run. She didn't think she could even stand.

Basil looked around, frightened for the first time. "I can't push you fast enough."

They could hear it now—footsteps, dozens of them, hundreds of them, all of them shuffling forward in lockstep. Basil hauled Amy from the chair and dragged her down an aisle, stashing her underneath a Petrichor dining table, away from the filthy rotting leviathan bearing down on them, making the floor shake, filling the air with its stink.

"Whatever happens," he whispered over the vast, soft, rotten noises that were getting louder, "don't help me. I can handle this. Just wait until they're gone, and then get out of here."

He walked back to the Bright and Shining Path, holding his cell phone above his head, a signal in the dark. Something in the shadows surged toward him. As it emerged out of the darkness Amy saw that it had hundreds of legs with filthy bare feet, packed so closely together they looked like they belonged to a single creature. She realized she was seeing an army, stretching off into the store. They were dressed in loose striped shirts and pants, their heads bowed forward, each man's forehead resting on the back of the neck of the man in front of him. They were standing so close that they looked like a great segmented centipede made of dead flesh. They stopped just a few feet in front of Basil.

Basil tried to look brave. He stood tall in the center of the Path, legs apart, silhouetted by the light of his phone. But then he saw them—he got a good, careful look at them—and whatever he had expected to see, it wasn't this. His expression faltered and he fell back on his training. "Orsk is closed for the evening. All of you are trespassing on private property."

For the briefest of moments, nothing moved.

Then his cell phone went into sleep mode, extinguishing the last glimmer of light from the Showroom, and the penitents fell upon him.

HANDLING A DISRUPTIVE PRESENCE

Here are the procedures to follow when finding a Disruptive Presence (DP) in your work environment.

❶ Assess

Is the DP alone?

Is the DP intoxicated?

Is the DP displaying physical aggression?

❷ Approach

Whenever possible, partner with another Team Leader for approach

Always approach in clear view of the DP

Stand no closer than six feet from the DP

❸ Announce

Clearly state your position at Orsk

Explain store guideline or policy the DP is violating

Request that the DP leave store immediately

REMEMBER: Safety of guests and store partners is paramount. Once their safety is secured, the secondary leadership objective is protecting money/merchandise.

12

ALBOTERK

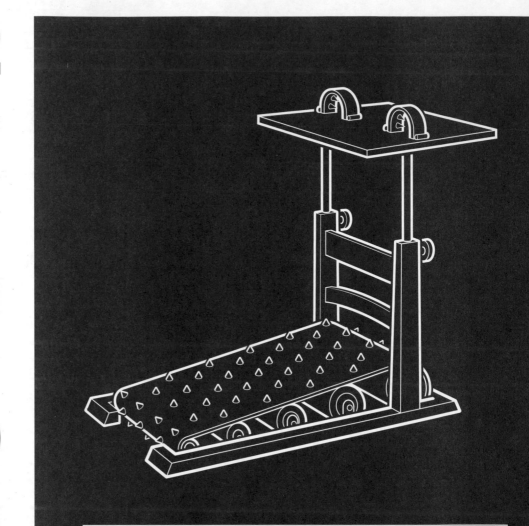

You can walk forever and never arrive, thanks to the infinite loop of the **ALBOTERK** treadwheel. A range of possibilities unfolds when you remove a destination from the equation and let the journey last forever.

AVAILABLE IN GRAY OAK, NATURAL BEECH, AND NIGHT OAK
W 22¾ X D 67¼ X H 49¼
ITEM NUMBER 8181666241

Amy made herself as small as possible. Her hope of being cured, her wish to have the warden find her, everything that had filled her head withered when she heard the noises coming from the Path. It was the sound of meat being pounded into pulp. She knew that she was a coward for not helping Basil, but she couldn't let them find her. She couldn't let them put her back in her chair. She dragged herself farther under the table, tucked herself into a ball, and waited for the noises to stop.

They went on for a very long time.

Even after the noises ceased and the army receded, dragging Basil away with them, Amy remained hidden underneath the table. She was tempted to stay there until dawn, until the floor lights automatically powered up and first shift arrived. It would be so much easier not to move. But Warden Worth was looking for her, and she knew it would be only a matter of time before the penitents came back, sweeping the floor, searching for her. She had no doubt they would find her, just as she knew Warden Worth was not a man who believed in forgiveness. She had to go. Now.

But to get out she needed light, and the only light was with Basil. She crawled on her hands and knees up the aisle, expecting at any moment for a hand to come out of the darkness and grab the back of her neck. The flooring ended and she felt the lip of the Bright and Shining Path. It was gritty now, smeared with mud and sand and something sticky. A marshy odor hung in the air. Amy swept her hands in big arcs across the grimy floor, searching for Basil's phone. The longer she searched, the more panic tightened her bruised chest. If she couldn't find the phone, she would have no light, and if she didn't have light she would have to creep through the store in the dark, wandering in circles, lost.

Her fingertips brushed something plastic that skidded away. *Got it*, she thought. She powered on the phone, and its dead television light bloomed in her face. She flashed it around to make sure nothing was waiting for her in the shadows, and then she studied the screen to find a way to brighten it.

It was locked with a passcode. Amy thought for a minute and then remembered Basil's devotion to Orsk. She spelled out the letters on his keypad, 6775, and to her delight the home screen opened. She thumbed through to the flashlight app, the light brightening as she punched it on.

Next Amy tried to stand, but her legs were bags of snapped twigs. She fell almost immediately, bruising her left knee as it smacked into the floor. Her feet ached, the bones in her knees ground against one another, her joints creaked, her spine felt shattered, and it took an enormous effort to brace herself against a Sculpin and haul herself to her feet.

The best she could manage was a slow and painful limp, but it was good enough to get her down the Path and into Bedrooms and then Bathrooms and then Wardrobes. From there she could go through Children's, take the shortcut to Storage Solutions, Home Office, and Living Rooms, then reach the escalator and, finally, the front door. Assuming that no other barricades were blocking her way.

Amy allowed herself a quick flash of Basil's cell phone every few minutes to orient herself. Each time she turned it on, she expected to see some distorted face grinning at her in the dark, some pale twisted body coming out of the shadows. Maybe Warden Worth standing in the middle of the aisle, waiting patiently for her return.

But she made it to Home Office unchallenged. On her right were ranks of Smagma bookshelves lined with row after row of *Design Is Good* books, their shadows dancing as Basil's phone trembled in her hand. And there was her familiar info post with its familiar greeting: "Have a question? Just Orsk!" The pun felt painfully normal. It was the first landmark that reassured her she was moving in the right direction.

Amy turned right, heading deeper into Home Office. The next time she flashed the phone, she glimpsed movement in the distance. She pressed the device to her chest, concealing its light, and crouched as low as she could, bruised knees trembling as she squatted next to a Karezza.

Something was definitely moving up ahead—she could hear it. Up there in the darkness, a motor was churning. The Path went straight past the noise, and Amy knew she had no choice. If she wanted to get out, she would have to get closer.

Terror singing in her veins, she began to crawl on all fours down the Path. The machine got louder, and soon she could hear a raspy breathing, along with another less human noise, like something sticky being stepped on over and over. The motor was loud and the panting was louder, and there was something familiar about it. Unable to resist, Amy pulled Basil's cell phone away from her stomach and pointed it toward the sound. The darkness evaporated, and she saw an Alboterk treadmill desk. Its black belt was moving fast and its desktop was angled forward. On the treadmill, a deformed figure was struggling to keep up. Its back was bent beneath a heavy burden and its sneakers were falling apart; one sole had peeled loose and was slapping the belt like a dog's tongue lapping a bowl of water.

"Trinity?" Amy whispered.

Trinity's wrists were bound with packing tape to the front of the desk. One of her enormous black gear bags, crammed full of something heavy, was strapped over her shoulders. She looked back at Amy, her hair matted with sweat.

"I saw a ghost," Trinity mumbled. "I finally saw a ghost, but he didn't like me."

"Let me get you off this thing."

"I'll be well soon."

"Was it Josiah?" Amy asked.

Trinity smiled. "Warden Worth promised to cure

me."

Then her face crumpled and she began to cry.

"Hold on," Amy said.

She went to the front of the desk and tried to unwrap the tape. That's when she saw what had happened to Trinity's fingers. They were shattered. Bundles of broken pencils sticking out in every direction, bruised and purple where blood pooled beneath the skin. Amy found the end of the tape and unwrapped Trinity's hands carefully to avoid hurting her more, but Trinity didn't seem to notice.

Next Amy lifted the bag from Trinity's back and eased her mangled hands through the straps. It was so heavy that it twisted in Amy's arms and fell to the floor. The zipper split open and Orsk catalogs spilled out like entrails. Amy wrapped her arms around Trinity's waist and pulled her off the treadmill.

"No," Trinity said, struggling weakly.

"Shhh," Amy whispered, holding her.

If anyone had come to Orsk that morning and asked Amy if she and Trinity were friends, she would have answered "It's complicated." But pain and fear have a way of simplifying things. Trinity was lost in the same hell as Amy, only Basil wasn't there to save her. There was only Amy.

"No," Trinity chanted under her breath. "No, no, no, no, no."

"We're getting out of here," Amy said, trying to imitate Basil's confidence, putting her arms around the struggling girl. "I'm not going to leave you behind. I promise."

She reached around Trinity's waist and guided her along, both of them limping down the Bright and

Shining Path.

Amy whispered a monologue as they stumbled forward. She hoped the sound of her voice—a human voice—would be a comfort to Trinity. "Once we're down the escalator, we can use the manual release and open the front doors and then we'll be outside in the parking lot. We'll call for help and send people back here. Lots of people. You're going to be okay. Everyone's going to be okay. We just have to get out of here."

They arrived at the top of the escalator. Downstairs, a toxic orange glow flooded through the windows lining the front of the store. To Amy's light-starved eyes, it felt as bright as day.

Then Basil's phone rang.

She froze while the theme from *Doctor Who* played way too loudly.

Amy fumbled for the button and answered. "Hello?"

"Where've you been?"

"Matt?" she whispered. "Where are you?"

"I'm all turned around," Matt said. "I think I'm in Storage Solutions. I'm standing next to a Smagma."

"I'm by the escalator in Living Rooms," Amy said, feeling giddy. Matt was an extra person. Matt could help with Trinity. "You know how to get here?"

"I'm going after Trinity," he said.

"I've already got her," Amy said. "She's right here."

"I just saw her through the shortcut. She's heading for Wardrobes—"

"No, Matt, I've got her," Amy said. "She's standing right next to me. "

"I can't leave her in here alone."

Amy stuck the phone in Trinity's face. "Talk to him. Say something."

But Trinity stood still, unable to speak. Amy slapped the phone back to her ear.

"I can't leave her," Matt said.

"It's a trick," Amy said. "This place is tricking you."

"I'll call you right back. I'm going after her."

The line went dead. Amy tried to call his number back, but it rang and rang and then went to voicemail. She looked up to see Trinity staring at her.

"This is what it does. It tricks us," Amy said. Trinity didn't seem to hear. "We have to keep moving."

As she tried to figure out how to get Trinity down the frozen escalator, Amy's eye caught the row of ten headshots showing Orsk senior management, all lined up along the wall in identical black frames. Only now the ten images depicted "Josiah Worth, Warden." In the first picture, his eyes were scratched out. Next was one with his entire face slashed to ribbons, the glass in the frame shattered. Next to that was one with a water stain that had eaten away the image, leaving a white shapeless blur on his shoulders. And so it continued down the line, each photo just another mutilated version of Josiah's grinning face: eyeless, his mouth carved away to a black void, scratched with needles, charred, burned with acid.

Amy felt Trinity twist in her grip and break free. Fumbling, she snagged the girl's T-shirt with her fingers, catching her at the last second. Amy pulled and Trinity swung toward her so that her lolling face was directly in front of Amy's.

"Sick," Trinity said.

"Come on," Amy said, twisting her fingers tighter in Trinity's shirt. "Let's get out of here."

Trinity cocked her head, confused.

"No one's allowed to leave the Beehive," she said.

She leaned backward, pulling away from Amy, until her tattered T-shirt split down the middle, falling away from her body. Amy looked down at the scrap of T-shirt in her hand, then back up at Trinity as the girl ran toward Living Rooms, disappearing into the darkness.

"Trinity!" Amy shouted, forgetting herself.

But Trinity was gone. The store had swallowed her like a black stone dropped into a bottomless lake. Nearby, something heavy slammed into a wall, and a crash sounded as shelves toppled to the floor. Seized by panic, Amy ran down the escalator. Her feet stumbled over the metal treads and she gripped the rails to keep from falling. She could see the glass doors leading out to the parking lot, glowing orange under the sodium vapor lamps. On one of Amy's first days at Orsk, Pat had shown her how to manually open the doors in case of a power failure. A special release was built into the frame; she simply had to press it and then wedge her fingers between the doors and pry them apart.

A scream ripped through the dark. Ruth Anne's scream.

This place is tricking you, she reminded herself. That's what it does.

Orsk is all about scripted disorientation.

It wants you to surrender to a programmed experience.

Ruth Anne screamed again, an animal wail.

Someone was doing something unimaginable to her. Amy couldn't tell where the scream was coming from. It might have been coming from inside her own head.

They're trying to slow you down, she told herself. They're right behind you. They want to keep you here forever. They don't want you to get out.

She pressed the release button with her thumb, then jammed her sore fingers into the crack between the doors and forced them apart. Without motorized assistance, the panels parted reluctantly, pushing against her, jamming when the opening was only two feet wide. Warm air rushed in all around her, and Amy slipped out through the gap.

She was free.

13

KRAANJK

Embrace the simplicity of eternal repetition with **KRAANJK**, a rustic handle mounted on resistance gears to encourage eternal turning. Enter a meditative state of despair after one hundred turns, one thousand turns, even ten thousand turns. The only rule is that it never stops, even when your body does.

AVAILABLE IN IRON
W 13¾ X D 13¼ X H 13¼
ITEM NUMBER 4266637111

Amy didn't stop running until she'd reached the center of the vast, orange-lit parking lot. She caught her breath and looked around for cop cars, but the parking lot was empty.

"Oh, come on," she moaned. "Where the hell are you?"

Standing in the middle of the empty lot, she could see the headlights of the cars and trucks barreling down Route 77; she could even see the exit ramp leading down to the feeder road.

The address you gave me is invalid, the dispatcher had told her. *It means that, according to our system, the address doesn't—*

Doesn't what? Doesn't exist? How was that possible?

Amy ran around to the side of the building, her sneakers slapping warm asphalt, until she reached the distant side lot where partners were required to park their vehicles.

There was Ruth Anne's Jeep with its "My other car is a Harley" bumper sticker. Basil's Nissan Cube with its TARDIS1 license plate. There was a third car, a junked-up Subaru, that had to be Matt's or Trinity's. Then there was her sad Honda Civic, leaking oil.

But still no cops. She had no one but herself.

Amy fumbled her keys from her pocket and opened the Honda's door. The car buzzed at her, as if a door ajar was the most important problem in her life right now. *You're not abandoning them*, she told herself. *You're going to get help*. It was the smart thing to do. It was a good idea.

She locked the doors, started the engine, and pointed her car toward the exit. Then she floored the gas before she could change her mind, aiming for the feeder road that led to Route 77.

"Someone has to get out," she said to herself. "Someone has to get out and get help. It doesn't mean I'm running away . . ."

But she *was* running away. That's what Warden Worth's chair had taught her: she was always giving up, quitting early, walking away. It was so much easier not to try. The chair had made it so easy to surrender.

At the edge of the parking lot, Amy pressed on the brakes. From there, she watched the lights of the highway, the endless stream of cars and buses and tractor trailers. No doubt a police cruiser was out there looking for an exit its officers would never find.

She looked back at the store. From a distance it didn't seem menacing at all. It was just a big beige box made out of cheap materials plunked down in a sea of asphalt. Everything else was smoke and mirrors, a programmed experience. It was easier to see this reality from the outside. It was easy to forget on the inside. And her friends were still on the inside.

No, not her friends. They were store partners, not friends. There was a difference, she reminded herself.

But Basil had come back. She thought he'd just been repeating a bunch of Orsk propaganda about responsibility, but he'd actually *meant* it. He'd rescued her from the chair and faced an army of penitents to keep her safe.

And Matt had refused to leave without Trinity, and Ruth Anne wouldn't have left without any of them.

*They're not your friend*s, Amy told herself. *You don't have to do this. They're not your responsibility.* She closed her eyes and felt the throbbing bruises and cuts from the tranquilizing chair laddered up and down her body. Sitting in the driver's seat reminded her of being back in the chair, and she felt heavy and warm. It was safe with her eyes closed. Her car jerked forward and stalled as her foot slipped off the brake. Amy's eyes flew open. Before she could nod off again, she bit down on the tip of the finger that had lost its nail.

Pain screamed down her arm and woke her up completely. Here was the other option: the tranquilizing chair. It was always waiting for her. It always wanted her back. It always wanted her to quit again, to sit down and never get back up.

In the end, Amy thought, everything always comes down to those two choices: stay down or stand up.

She cut the wheel hard, drove back to the main entrance, and parked on a yellow-striped patch marked NO STOPPING OR STANDING. She walked to the main entrance and found that the doors had closed and dead-bolted themselves. Of course they had. Amy cupped her hands and peered up through the glass at the Showroom floor. She could see the shadows coiling around in the darkness, skittering through the aisles, dripping down the walls. The Creepy Crawlies wanted to be left alone with Ruth Anne, Matt, Trinity, and Basil. Amy had gotten away. They didn't want her back.

But hadn't Basil said that the door to the partners' entrance was still broken? She jogged around the side of the building and yanked on the door. It swung open easily, and in the orange light from the parking lot she could see the time clock on the opposite wall frozen at 3:15 a.m. Just looking into the store again was enough to make her heart race. This was her last chance to turn back. This was her last chance to act like a smart person. She could smell the sour, swampy stink of the store, and the air pouring out the door was cold and stagnant. Before she could change her mind, she stepped inside.

Her first stop would be the break area. That was where they'd all promised to regroup. Even if no one was there, she could find flashlights, first-aid kits, useful things. Holding up Basil's cell phone to light her way, she turned it to the left and saw the base of the stairs leading up to the second floor. Amy forced herself to head toward them and then jumped when the door behind her slammed shut, sealing her inside.

Basil's cell phone cast a watery digital glow over the walls as Amy made her way to the stairs, her senses hyperalert. At the top she turned down a hallway lined with office doors. Each was hiding something, each was on the verge of swinging open and showing her something she didn't want to see. In the cell phone's glow, she saw that the walls were riddled with cracks, weeping water, their paint bubbling, flaking, sloughing off and peeling to the floor in drifts.

Something darted across the floor—another rat, wet and filthy, racing along the edge of the wall and vanishing into darkness. Amy forced herself to calm down. Rats were the least of her worries right now. They were just more scripted disorientation. She breathed deeply and continued down the hallway. And then she heard it. A gentle scrape from behind one of the doors.

There is no point in being scared anymore, Amy told herself as she watched her hand reach for the handle and turn the knob. The door swung open. Inside was a supply closet filled with reams of paper and black markers, staplers and printer ink cartridges, everything lined up in neat and orderly stacks on the shelves.

But at the bottom of the back wall, a hole had been torn in the drywall. It was surrounded by scratches, the edges smeared with something dark. A cold rancid wind vented from the void, and something on the floor caught her eye. Amy knelt down and picked it up. A small tube of Blistex Medicated Berry lip balm. Amy dropped it and backed into the hall.

She had a feeling that the break area was going to be empty when she got there, and she was right. The first thing she did was open the first-aid kit bolted to the wall beside the door. Relief washed over her when she saw the yellow flashlight clipped inside. She yanked it out and clicked it on, and suddenly the room was full of daylight. Amy slid Basil's cell phone into her pocket and ran her flashlight over the walls. She checked under the Arsle tables, just to be sure. No rats, no men in striped pajamas, no Matt, no Ruth Anne, no Trinity. No Basil. Something cold and wet touched her skull, and she ducked to escape it. Whirling around with the flashlight revealed more shadows. Something small and silver dropped in front of her.

Amy looked up and gasped, then pressed herself to the wall, as far from the center of the room as possible. The stain on the ceiling had grown. It was a huge pregnant bulge, ripe with yellow water, dripping into a vast puddle in the center of the room. It looked like it was going to rupture at any moment. Runnels of dirty water chattered eagerly down the walls, into the bucket of Magic Tools, streaming over stacks of waterlogged Orsk catalogs, or what used to be Orsk catalogs. Now they were toppled and mixed with yellowing ledger paper filled with precise handwriting. The top sheet was dated May 5, 1839:

> . . . in short, this commission found that the Cuyahoga Panopticon is nothing more than a mill for the manufacture of Lunatics. Many of the Penitents have lost their minds in the numbing grind of repetitive labor; others have given in to Despair and disfigured themselves. The Treadwheel has been disconnected from its grinding stone, Penitents who should be employed in gainful labor are sent to "The Crank" until they become too injured to continue—and there is no gainful industry to be observed. Warden

Josiah Worth is not only aware of this situation; but seems to revel in it. Our recom-
mendation is the Immediate Closure . . .

Amy dropped the paper. This information was
nothing she didn't already know. There was nothing
left to see here, no one was coming; it was time to
move on. She took one last glance around the room
and noticed that the sign on the wall had changed.
Its message used to be "The hard work makes Orsk
your family, and the hard work is free." But the running water had worn away many of the letters. Now, it
simply read: "Work makes you free."

She was nearly out the door when she heard whis-
pering. Someone was close by, a mumbling scratching
on her eardrums. She flicked the flashlight around,
but she was alone. Then she pressed her ear to the wet
wall and whispered, "Hello?"

The reply was so loud, she jumped back.

" . . . hide, hiding, can't find me, can't see me, keep
going . . . "

The voice was harsh and sibilant. Amy recognized
it instantly. "Ruth Anne?"

Something thumped and rustled on the other side
of the drywall. "Amy?"

She pressed her hands to the wall, her fingers
clawing helplessly at the paint. "Ruth Anne," she said.
"I'm going to get you out of there."

"No," Ruth Anne whispered back. "They can't see
me in here."

"Who can't see you?"

"The Creepy Crawlies."

"Did you get in through the closet?"

"I made a hiding place," Ruth Anne said.

Something sharp scraped against the other side of the wall. It sounded like fingernails, and then Amy remembered the hole scratched in the closet wall and the dark fluid smeared around it.

"Are you hurt?" Amy asked.

"It hurt at first," Ruth Anne said. "It hurt a lot. But now they can't find me."

"Go back to the hole," Amy said, pressing her palms against the wall. "Can you find your way back to the closet? I'll meet you there—"

THUD!

Something slammed into the other side of the wall, knocking Amy back. Ruth Anne gabbled in fear. "They're coming!"

"The hole! Meet me at the hole!"

Amy ran back to the supply closet. She didn't see how she could fit through, but if Ruth Anne could make it, then so could she. She crouched down, ready to crawl through, only to discover that something was already crawling out. A hand, black with grime, wrapped its fingers around the lip of the opening.

"Help me," Ruth Anne whispered.

"Give me your other hand," Amy said.

She grabbed both of Ruth Anne's wrists and knew immediately that something was wrong. Ruth Anne's arms were slick with blood and gore, and Amy could barely get a grip. She wiped her palms on her jeans and tried again, pulling harder, guiding Ruth Anne's head and shoulders through the opening. "It's going to be okay," Amy reassured her. "You'll be home on the couch watching *Real Housewives* in no time. No more Creepy Crawlies."

Amy felt something wrong with Ruth Anne's fingertips. They were hard like calluses but the nails were missing and all the surrounding flesh was raw. In gouging out a hole, Ruth Anne had worked her fingers to the bone, literally. Each digit ended in a bloody white tip.

"Amy!" Ruth Anne screamed.

Something had her. She was being yanked backward, back into the hole. Amy grabbed her by the shoulders, but whatever was pulling from inside the wall was too strong.

"Hold on," Amy said.

"I don't want to see them!" Ruth Anne gibbered.

"I won't let you go!" Amy said.

She braced her feet against the wall and leaned back, but Ruth Anne was slipping from her grip, sinking back into the hole, sinking into darkness.

"Help me!"

Amy dove through the hole headfirst.

Behind the wall was a cramped passage framed by drywall and metal ductwork. It was too low to crawl on all fours; Amy inched forward on her belly, using her feet to propel herself.

Ruth Anne was sliding backward, her bloodied hands slapping at the aluminum ducts and failing to find purchase. Amy lunged forward, grabbing her wrists with both hands. The flashlight rolled away, strobing through the passage.

"I got you," she said. "I won't let go, I swear."

Ruth Anne just shook her head. Suddenly her voice was calm, as if she'd experienced a rush of clarity about her fate. "You're not strong enough."

"Yes, I am."

"No, you're not. There's one of you and too many of them. But I want you to know something, sweetheart. This is not your fault."

Whatever was pulling Ruth Anne pulled harder, yanking her wrists from Amy's grasp, dragging her deeper into the darkness. Amy wriggled forward but she wasn't fast enough; she couldn't keep up.

"Ruth Anne!" she yelled.

Her friend didn't seem concerned at all. She was no longer resisting; she had stopped trying to fight back. "Don't you worry," Ruth Anne said. "If I can't see them, they can't see me."

Then without hesitation she hooked her bony fingertips into her eye sockets and raked them down her face.

"No!" Amy screamed.

She grabbed her flashlight and aimed it into the crawl space but it was too late: Ruth Anne was gone. All that remained were bloody handprints on the drywall. And the sound of a lifeless corpse being pulled deeper into the store.

Ruth Anne had hugged her that morning when she thought she'd been fired. Snoopy was sitting on the sofa waiting for her to get home and watch TV. She hadn't hesitated when Carl was hurting himself, she'd just stripped off her blouse and tried to stop the bleeding. Ruth Anne had been the best of them.

Something hardened inside Amy and she promised herself she would get the others out. All of them. It didn't matter what tried to stop her or what she had to go through. She'd quit on enough things in her life—she wasn't going to quit on this. Whatever had happened to Ruth Anne wasn't going to happen to anyone else.

Amy hauled herself out of the hole, scraping the skin off her ribs as she went. She closed the supply closet door gently behind her and made her way through the back of house until she reached the swinging double doors that led to the café. She switched off the flashlight and pushed open one of the doors, slipping out onto the floor. In front of her, in the orange glow from the café windows on her right, Amy could make out the elevator and stairwell leading down to the Market Floor. Children's was to her left, and she could see just enough of its shadowy shapes to navigate by.

Her guard was down, so when something moved to her right, Amy clicked on the flashlight and pointed it into the café. The first thing she saw was a man's back. He was wearing a rough gray coat with wide stripes running across it. As she watched, the figure reached with both arms to his right and took an Arsle café chair from the man next to him. They held it by the legs, at chest height, and passed it along as though they were ferrying furniture out of a friend's house. Then the man passed the chair to another man on his left, who passed it to another, and another, and another, all the way around the ring.

The sheer number of them took her breath away. She counted twenty-one before stopping; if there were more, she didn't want to know. The men were ignoring her, passing around at least a dozen chairs in a circle, working rhythmically, mechanically, like pistons in a machine. Something moved in the darkness of the stairwell and Amy swung her flashlight toward it. Four of the shadow people were coming up the stairs.

They were not quite as scrawny or filthy as the men in the café. They wore hoods, and from their belts swung truncheons; they advanced on her as inexorably as robots. Amy knew they were the warders, the guards, the ones who chased down escapees and disciplined troublemakers. She knew they were coming for her.

Amy had taken her eyes off the men in the café for only a second, but when she turned back they had placed their chairs on the floor and were all staring at her.

The saliva in her mouth went dry and her stomach filled with acid. If she had been able to gather her wits she would have run, but she felt stunned by the full force of the men's attention.

Their faces were the worst. They were smeared, obscured, covered in a black veil, as if something had smudged their features with a dirty eraser, leaving nothing behind but indistinct knobs of shadow. No eyes, no mouth, no nose, no humanity; their individuality rubbed out.

Amy looked back at the stairs. The hooded men had reached the landing. Galvanized by their proximity, she turned toward Children's and ran.

She snapped off the flashlight, hoping the darkness would hide her. She could hear bodies moving behind her, chasing her, but she didn't risk turning around. She knew exactly where she needed to go. Darting and ducking around furniture, she passed through the dark burrows of Children's, raced into the shadowy towers of Wardobes, skipped past Bathrooms, at last making her way to a Finnimbrun bedroom display. She dipped her flashlight to the floor and scanned the beam around. The ground was covered with dirt, smears of mud, and clots of black filth forming a trail past the Mesonxic closet organization system. Right back where she started. Opposite the closet, at the end of the narrow rust-colored hallway, a fake wooden door gaped like a clown's mouth, inviting her inside.

Basil was back there. Maybe Matt and Trinity, too. It was too late for Ruth Anne, but Amy could still save *someone*. She had to go. Forcing herself to breathe deeply, filling both lungs with the rank marshy stench that came wafting on the cold air spilling from the open door, she ran inside, flicking her flashlight beam around the walls as she entered the heart of the Beehive.

JODLÖPP

14

A slow and steady step and an attentive erect posture are firmly encouraged when you wear this crippling iron cap. Giving your skull and neck the weight they need to bow into a permanent attitude of submission, **JODLÖPP** features a bell that will let everyone know you've arrived.

AVAILABLE IN IRON
W 18¾ X D 14¼ X H 16¼
ITEM NUMBER 3927272666

Somehow the corridor had narrowed since her last visit, and the smell of rancid rot filled Amy's head. Her flashlight swept the passage, lighting it from floor to ceiling, chasing the shadows away. The plaster on the crumbling walls was soaked and rotten like leprous skin, the gritty floor was soft and damaged. The ceiling glistened with stalactites of dirty water and slime.

Amy ran down the passage. Up ahead it turned right, disappearing into darkness. When she reached the corner, she hesitated and then stuck her flashlight around, followed by her head. The corridor lay quiet and expectant, waiting for her. After another thirty feet, the passage split into a T. Amy turned left, guided by instinct more than anything. She turned left, then right, then right, then left again, moving deeper and deeper into the Beehive.

The corridor narrowed even further until eventually her shoulders were brushing against the walls.

She listened carefully for voices, hoping to hear Basil or Matt or Trinity. But all she heard was the gentle drip of water trickling down the walls and pooling at her feet. Claustrophobia was creeping in, and within her gut she felt the cold certainty that if she tried to retrace her steps, the corridors behind her would not be the same.

Scripted disorientation, she reminded herself. *Keep moving.*

Right, left, left, right.

A needle of cold water fell from the ceiling and slid down the back of her neck, jolting her like an electric shock. She reached to wipe it away. The liquid was swirled with yellow filth, like pus from a lanced boil. The weight of the walls pressed in around her, making the air heavy to breathe, giving her a headache.

Left, right, right, left.

Amy turned a corner and froze. She had arrived in a different sort of corridor, one without the weeping plaster walls. The passage was lined on both sides with tall iron grates like doors, two feet wide and crisscrossed with flaking bars. She wasn't sure what to do. Cold water tapped her hair, urging her forward. There was no telling if the grates were unlocked, or if anything hid in the darkness behind them. But she felt certain she was getting closer. The store had tried to keep her from finding this place; it had tried to confuse her, but she'd found it anyway.

She took a step forward, then another.

"Basil?" she whispered. "Matt? Trinity?"

Up ahead on the left, a pale white worm squirmed out of a grate. Amy stepped closer and realized it was a finger. Human hands were creeping out of the grates, squeezing through the gaps and straining toward her, sensing her warmth. Filthy digits waved in the cold air like sea anemones, their fingerpads sniffing her out.

Amy swept the corridor with her flashlight, and the grates erupted with pale flesh as hundreds of hands pushed themselves through the bars, the walls alive with fingers like living hair. As Amy dashed down the hallway, they scraped across her face, her thighs, her hips, her breasts. They tried to hook her clothing and burrow through to her skin.

The passage ended in another T. To the left, Amy saw more of the same—more grates and hundreds of writhing hands. She went right. The water was dripping faster now, falling down like rain. Amy wiped her face with her sleeve. She rounded another corner— she was now totally and completely lost but knew she was getting closer to something. This new corridor had much larger rooms spaced much farther apart. She forced herself to aim the flashlight into each one. They all had furniture dragged in from the Showroom floor, as if the penitents were insects stocking their hive for winter. Inside one was a Kummerspeck desk with a chair arranged neatly behind it. In another, a Skoptsy futon mattress, vile with mildew, sagged against a wall. Still another featured smashed glass mixing bowls, the shards glittering in her flashlight beam and forming a thick carpet waiting to open veins and arteries.

The last room at the end of the corridor was equipped with the Mungo Towel Rack System. It consisted of two brushed steel bars, each with an attractively streamlined curve: an upper bar for large towels and a lower thinner bar for hand towels and wash-cloths. It was one of the best sellers in Bathrooms and here it was with a man's body hanging from it. His wrists were bound behind him, strapped to the top bar with leather thongs. His legs were bent and his feet were crossed one over the other and tied to the lower rack so that his body formed a grotesque sagging arc. A Widdiful pillowcase, dripping with dark fluids, was pulled over his head like a hood. Amy instantly recognized the shirt and pants. The figure stirred, and she heard the soft muffled sound of a bell.

"Basil?" she whispered.

He made a low, pained groan and thrashed from side to side, the bell unnaturally loud in the tiny room.

"It's me," Amy said. "It's okay. I came back."

She pinched the top of the pillowcase between two fingers and snatched it off his head. Steel straps were clamped around his skull, forming a cage held in place with iron screws and locked around his neck by a bolt. A crude metal bell hung from the collar. One of Basil's eyes was swollen nearly shut. The other was caked with blood. His lower lip was split, and his cheekbones were bruised and swollen. He turned his pulped face toward Amy, trying to place her.

"M'my?" he mumbled.

"I'm going to get you down," she said.

Basil started panting in great bursts. Amy studied the leather thongs tying his wrists. They had been stretched so tight that their knots were like steel. Then she saw that Basil's weight had pulled out the screws on one side of the Mungo base plate. She pressed the sole of her shoe against the wall, yanked on the bar, and Basil's weight did the rest. He fell face first onto the floor, catching it on his shoulder and neck, howling in pain as the bell jangled wildly.

With the tension off his bonds, Amy was able to pick apart the knots. She slipped his feet through the leather loops and gently lowered them to the floor. More complicated was the cage locked around his skull; she tried twisting the bolt threaded through the collar and gasped with relief when it started to turn. After that, it was a simple matter of spinning it loose, opening the hasp, and flinging it across the cell.

Freed from its weight, Basil lay in a tangled heap, panting, with hot tears running down his face.

"I'm going to turn you over," Amy said.

When she rolled him onto his side, he gasped. Amy grabbed his arms, pulling them out from underneath his body. She rubbed his wrists, trying to restore sensation. "Can you hear me?" she asked.

"My arm," Basil asked. "Is it broken?"

Amy had no idea. She didn't know what a broken arm looked like.

"We're getting out of here," she said. "The store will try to stop us. It'll disorient you, get inside your head, try to confuse you and control you. But if you stay focused, you can block it out. You have to *fight*, do you understand?"

Basil looked pained. He closed his eyes.

"I told you to go," he said.

"When have I ever done what you told me?" Amy said.

Basil made a face, and Amy couldn't tell what it was. His lips stretched tightly over his bloody teeth and his cheeks and forehead crinkled up. She realized he was smiling.

"S'responsible," he muttered.

"What's that?"

He cleared his throat and spat out blood. "You're Shop Responsible," he said. "I knew it."

With Amy's help, Basil pushed himself into a seated position and leaned against the wet plaster wall.

"It was the warden," he whispered. "Josiah Worth. He did this to me. He said I was weak, ineffective. He said he would manage the people in my care."

"You're a fine manager, Basil."

He shook his head. "Where's Trinity?"

"She's hurt," Amy said. "But she's still in the store. Matt's trying to find her."

"He's safe?"

"Not really," Amy said. She hesitated, not sure she could say the next part out loud. "I think Ruth Anne is gone."

"Gone how?"

"Dead," she said.

Amy swallowed and felt a piece of glass in her throat.

Basil rested his head against the wall and squeezed his eyes shut. "I knew I shouldn't have brought her here tonight. I knew it. I got her killed. I screwed up and got Ruth Anne killed."

"It's not your fault," Amy said. "This is no one's fault."

Basil shook his head.

"It was my choice," he said. "I brought you both here. It gave me an excuse to talk to you."

"What?" Amy asked.

"I thought I could figure out why you're popular,"

Basil said. "Why everyone talks to you."

"I'm not that popular," Amy said.

"I'm boring," Basil said. "I had to become a floor manager before anyone would talk to me."

Amy thought about it for a minute.

"There are worse things than being boring," she finally said.

They sat there for so long that Amy thought Basil had fallen asleep.

"We need to go," she said. "You can rest when we're outside."

She tried to help him up, but Basil didn't seem anxious to brave the Showroom floor again and Amy knew she had to motivate him. "You've got a sister waiting for you. She needs you to come home, right?"

"Her birthday's tomorrow," Basil said. "Today actually, I guess."

"What's her name?"

"Shawnette. She'll be ten."

"What did you get her?"

"Legos," he said. "She wants an iPad, but we're on a budget."

"And a cake? Did you buy her a cake?"

"Gonna make one. It's a thing we do. Tradition."

"Then we better get you out of here," Amy said. "We better get you home so you can bake your cake."

"One more minute," Basil said. "Just let me rest for one more minute."

Amy sat beside him. Her flashlight was dying, yellowing to the color of old bone. All right: one more minute. It felt good just to sit, to not be moving, to not be running. It felt good and it felt right. They could stay here and be safe until the morning crew found them. There was no need to be scared, or to make any more difficult decisions. Her flashlight grew dimmer and dimmer. Eventually it would die and they could sit in the dark and wait.

Another part of Amy's mind knew this wasn't true. This was the building thinking for her. Worming its way inside her head, dredging up old habits and old fears. She reached down to her missing fingernail and squeezed it hard until she saw bright stars flashing in her field of vision. The pain got her on her feet and thinking clearly. She clapped her hands, the sound echoing harshly against the walls of the room. "No more stopping," she said. "We can't stop until we're out."

Basil looked up, groggy. "Just one more minute."

"No," she said, grabbing an arm and hauling him to his feet. "This is how the store wins. When we stop trying, when we're lazy. Come on, Basil. Move it."

She felt like a gym teacher, clapping and cajoling, pulling and threatening, but she finally got Basil to his feet.

"Whoa," he said thickly through smashed lips, staggering to the right.

Amy caught him under his ribs and held him up while blood surged back into his legs, sending pins and needles cascading down his calves and into his feet. Basil hunched in pain and Amy helped him stand until it passed.

"Which way?" he asked.

"Follow me," she said with great confidence, even though she was completely lost. She remembered someone telling her that the way out of every maze was to follow the wall on the right. It wasn't much of a plan but it was something to focus on, a goal that would keep the store out of her head.

She helped Basil hobble out of the cell, but at the door his legs gave out and he went down.

"It's cold," he moaned.

In the dim glow, Amy saw that his bare feet were wet. A thin scrim of water was rushing across the floor, flowing down the hall. Small cataracts were forming around his heels.

"Something spilled," she said.

"Broken pipe," Basil corrected as she helped him to his feet.

He was right. More water was coming, surging along the floor. It was only an inch deep at most, but it showed no sign of letting up. They began to walk quicker, their footsteps echoing down the hall.

"How do we get out of here?" Basil asked.

Amy was about to explain her labyrinth proposal when she had a better idea: "We'll follow the water," she said. "Water always finds a way out."

Freezing air rose up from the water as they splashed down the hall and rounded a corner, returning to one of the corridors lined with grates. A sea of hands reached through the bars, agitated by their arrival, grasping at their scent.

"What the hell?" Basil asked.

Amy handed him the dying flashlight. "Keep it pointed forward and stay close."

"There's too many of them," he said.

"I don't see a lot of options," Amy said. "You going to quit on me?"

Basil shook his head. Before he could change his mind, Amy grabbed his belt and entered the gauntlet.

The hands came at her fast, albino bats flapping out of the dark, snapping at her face. Snatching hands, grabbing hands, pinching hands. Amy put her head down and forged through the whirlwind. Hands grabbed her hair and tore out chunks; they wormed their way into her mouth, hooked her cheeks, snatched at her clothes, slapped her eyes, sending white light strobing inside her skull, trying to knock her off balance, trying to pull her to them.

Stumbling, shaking, whimpering, covered in filth from the dirty hands, she staggered forward, dragging Basil behind her by the belt. She tried to slap the forest of hands out of the way, but they snatched at her fingers and cracked her knuckles as they tore at her face. And then they were gone.

Amy and Basil stumbled out like swimmers reaching the beach, and both of them stood at the end of the hall gasping and panting. Basil's eyes were wide and glassy, fixed on the floor, his shredded lips moving soundlessly. The hands had reopened his wounds and he was bleeding freely. Amy let go of his belt and bent over, feeling dirty.

"Your hair?" Basil said. "They ripped it out."

Amy raised her arms and felt her scalp. It was sticky with blood. Something cold touched her feet and she jumped. The water was soaking into her Chuck Taylors. "Just keep moving," she said. "We're almost there."

They went left and right and right again, always following the flow of the water. Amy knew that more water meant they were moving in the right direction; water always followed the path of least resistance. Her flashlight could barely cut through the shadows anymore, it was just a glow that dimly reflected off the surface of the surging black current. Despite his injuries, Basil kept up with her; when he fell behind, she grabbed his good arm and pulled, and the pair kept scurrying forward. *Like rats fleeing a sinking ship*, Amy thought.

Finally they rounded yet another corner, and there, twenty feet ahead, was the back of a cheap white wooden door. It was the way out to the Showroom. Water was pooling in front of it and Amy sloshed forward, turned the cold knob, and pushed. The door swung open and the water cascaded out, spreading across Bedrooms, disappearing beneath Pykonnes and Finnimbruns.

"A flooded Showroom," Basil muttered, collapsing onto a display bed. "Corporate is going to love it."

"That's the least of our worries," Amy said, taking the flashlight from him. Then she saw what Basil was sitting on. "Bedrooms," she said. "We're in Bedrooms. Come on."

She raced off, taking the light with her. Basil followed. Her feeble flashlight flickered and guttered like a candle. Amy raised it high then swung it low, crawling over beds.

"What are you looking for?" Basil asked.

"The bags," she said. "Matt's gear bag had flashlights."

"This place is huge, Amy," Basil said. "There's no way you're going to find them."

Amy stopped darting around and zeroed in on her target. She flung herself over the Müskk, reached down behind it, and hauled up a dripping black duffle bag.

"You were saying?" she said.

Jamming her arms into the zippered mouth, she rummaged around and then turned it upside down and shook it over the bed. Out fell a long black Maglite.

Basil seized it and clicked it on. A powerful beam of white light lanced out.

"You are my new superhero," he said to Amy. "Now come on, we have to find the others."

Basil swept his light across Bedrooms.

"Stop!" Amy shouted.

It was too late. The arc of the beam showed what was around them. The filthy ghosts, hundreds of them, scattered through the furniture. Everywhere Basil's light landed were more penitents, waiting for them with infinite patience, surrounding them, filling the Showroom floor.

Amy remembered being grabbed and carried off to her chair, and a spear of pure terror struck her spine, rooting her to the ground. Hundreds of these un-men with their smudged faces encircled them, motionless, not breathing, corpse still, dead silent. Then a disturbance came from somewhere within their mass—a cluster of figures shuffled to one side, making way for someone bubbling up within their ranks. Finally the figure emerged from the colorless crowd of the dead: Carl, or rather Warden Josiah Worth, dabbing a fabric sample at his lips, his face a twisted leer of pure hatred.

NUMBER	NAME	OFFENSE	SENTENCE
00314	Harold Asher	Vagabonding and barratry	~~3 years~~ 4 years

TREATMENT: His degenerate aspect and sallow features caused me to assign to him seven hours on the Tread Wheel each day. His sickly aspect increases. But I suspect him of malingering. Nothing is so certain as that the evils of idleness can be shaken off by hard work.

NUMBER	NAME	OFFENSE	SENTENCE
00315	Leon Bultz	Consorting with low women and public inebriation	~~2 years~~ ~~3 years~~ 4 years

TREATMENT: A daily dose of Mercury has calmed him greatly. Those who sow no seeds reap no reward.

NUMBER	NAME	OFFENSE	SENTENCE
00316	Osborne Goldberg	Threatening behavior	3 years

TREATMENT: This sallow fellow seems to be quite ill, suffering from true lunacy and bearing all the physical signs of degeneracy. We have prescribed to him the Iron Cap to be worn at all times, and when he becomes agitated, a few hours on the rotational board encourages him to swoon and purge himself of vile fluids. Amid an eternal heritage of sorrow and suffering our work begins.

NUMBER	NAME	OFFENSE	SENTENCE
00317	Matthew Sweagan	Petty larceny with partial verdict	~~4 years~~ 5 years

TREATMENT: Sentenced to workhouse where his abusive temperament required him to be ~~removed~~ remanded into my care. Prescribed ten thousand turns of the crank each day. Notice that flesh of his hands has begun to slough off and become full of pus. For his health, we have removed his thumbs. He is now returned to the crank.

15

LITTABOD

Using the power of centrifugal force to cause blackouts and unconsciousness, **LITTABOD** is a ceaseless rotational machine that harnesses the primal forces of nature and turns them against your body. If you're lucky, you'll simply experience vomiting and permanent brain damage.

AVAILABLE IN SNOW BIRCH, NIGHT BIRCH, AND GRAY OAK
W 92¾ X D 32¼ X H 34¼
ITEM NUMBER 6595956661

Amy's first instinct was to switch off her light, tuck her head under her arms like a little girl, and make them go away. As if they were merely Ruth Anne's Creepy Crawlies. If she didn't see them, they wouldn't see her. But she knew it was too late for that. She couldn't hide anymore. They were real. So she forced herself to look.

She saw a gallery of rotten and humiliated flesh. Arms hung at obscene angles, legs were twisted and shattered at the knee, spines gnarled and bent, their rags and flesh hanging in tatters, caked with reeking mud. She couldn't take her eyes off them.

"Work burns the sickness from a man's mind," Warden Worth proclaimed. "It is the philosopher's stone that transmutes the base metal of deviancy into the pure gold of obedience."

It was the same kind of hellfire and brimstone sermon as before—only this time Amy noticed something wrong with Josiah's voice. It sounded far away, as if she and Basil were listening over a bad phone connection. Even worse, the sounds of his speech were out of sync with the movement of his lips. He looked like a character in a badly dubbed movie.

"I think we can run for it," Amy whispered to Basil. "Over on the left."

He didn't answer. She turned and saw that his skin was greasy with cold sweat, and he was muttering under his breath.

"My children," said the warden, smiling at them. "The coward and the fool. What a disappointment that the two of you have not yet grasped my lesson. But I am a tireless instructor, and now you shall join your fellows in my mill where we will grind your minds into a shape more pleasing."

"Your mill is closed," Amy said. "It doesn't exist anymore."

"Poor sick wretch," Josiah said. "I want to make you well. My penitents came to me riddled with corruption and I worked their mortal bodies to effect a cure. Some were harmed in the refinement of their minds, some were forced into painful new shapes, but mustn't the sculptor crack the stone to pull from within it a more pleasing form? Must the surgeon cease his cutting at the first cries of pain?"

"We're leaving," Amy said. "We're taking our friends and getting out of here."

"I would be violating my oath if I let you go while you are still so sick," the warden continued. "My patrons could apprehend neither my methods nor my mission, and so they tried to snatch my penitents away before they were cured. I could not let that happen then and I will not let it happen now."

Amy looked at the water on the floor and a realization dawned. "What did you do?" she asked.

"You would do better to ask how I saved them. I made the ultimate sacrifice. My warders took them to the basement workrooms, and we locked the doors. The ones who would not cooperate were gently shut up inside coffins so they would not disturb the others. Then I opened the sluice gates and let the river sing them to sleep, as a mother takes a sick babe into her arms."

"You drowned them," Amy said.

"I hid them in the curtains of time. All three hundred and eighteen of them. I pulled the river over their heads like a veil, and then I opened my own throat and waited until I could bring them back and cure them. I understand it caused much inconvenience to my sponsors. I understand they could not find the bodies and had to pack coffins with river mud and bury them to quiet the mewling families. But I have outlasted them all. These sick men—sick with laziness, sick with misunderstanding, sick with lunacy, sick with deviancy—they shall be cured. I will not cease my labors until they are made whole, even if I must begin my work afresh every night until the end of time. Is that not a commitment worthy of celebration? Is not my mind magnificent?"

As he shrieked and crowed, Amy looked at the man-shapes surrounding them. Their faces were obscured, draped with filth and darkness, but she didn't feel that they were evil. Instead she felt a profound sorrow for them. These prisoners had served their sentences long ago. These poor lost souls, never paroled, never resting, doomed to repeat the same pointless tasks over and over. They hadn't put her in the chair because they hated her. They had put her in the chair because they didn't know what else to do with her. Their guilt had kept them enslaved to this place long after their sentences had been served.

"I regret you could not be cured in one night," Warden Worth said, looking at Amy. "But your disease has reached an advanced stage. It will be a difficult procedure."

"I don't have a disease," Amy said.

"Oh, but you do. And now you shall join your friends. It is good to have new patients, for there are so many cures I have yet to try. Dr. Cotton's Theory of Organ Removal. The Rotational Machine. Hydrotherapy Baths. Total Immersion."

"Listen to me," Amy shouted, raising her voice and projecting across the Showroom. "You don't have to be here anymore."

The shapes gave no indication of having heard her.

"Amy?" Basil hissed. "What the hell are you doing?"

"But ultimately we shall rely on toil," the warden was saying. Amy didn't know whether it was her imagination or whether his voice was getting louder, as if he was trying to drown her out. "It will be the backbone of your cure. For toil is the great grinding stone to make keen the blade of your spirit. Toil is the ladder by which your putrid flesh ascends into health."

"You have served your time!" Amy continued. "Any sentence you had is long over. What did you do? Kill people who would be dead now anyway? Steal food for your families who are already in the ground? Owe money to a company that has been out of business for a hundred years? You've paid for your crimes."

"Beware the words of liars who lure you into weakness!" Warden Worth shouted. "You know the weight of your own sin, which shall never be relieved. Expiation unto eternity. That is the only path to wellness, the only true command."

"No one's keeping you here," Amy said. "You're not chained, you're not sick, you don't need a cure. You can walk away at any time. That's all you have to do. Walk away. You can be free!"

A muddy restlessness passed through the penitents.

"I don't think this is a good idea," Basil whispered.

"Free!" Amy said, doubling down. "This isn't a prison anymore. It collapsed decades ago. Its walls are gone. No one remembers your crimes!"

"Freedom through work!" Warden Worth screamed, hysterical. "That is the only freedom! For work is the whip that mortifies your failed flesh and shapes your sins into something more pleasing, something more—"

"You aren't in chains anymore!" Amy shouted over him. "Your sentences are just habits. You've been free for decades—you just never realized it!"

"She's a liar!" Josiah shrieked. "She's filling you with honeyed words and false hope. Tonight has but one conclusion. There are no other paths to travel. There is only one end."

There was silence for a moment, a second when Amy felt that anything could happen. Then Warden Worth stumbled forward, shoved from behind. Splashing across the wet floor, he whirled around.

"Who dares touch me?" he shouted. "I am your

keeper!"

The crowd of shadows was shuffling forward now. They surrounded him with their muddy bodies and then seized him and began to pull him and push him, shoving him from one side of their tight circle to the other. They were hungry, like a pack of wild animals. Something had been unleashed. The penitents swarmed around him, thick and heavy with rot and grime, blocking him from sight. Josiah squealed through his torn throat. As his screams turned to liquid burbling, Amy was glad she couldn't see the rest.

She and Basil turned to leave, but a cluster of penitents stood in the way, as still as stones. "Why aren't they moving?" Basil whispered.

"I don't know," Amy whispered back. "Head left."

They edged to the left, toward the Bright and Shining Path, but more penitents blocked their passage. It didn't make sense, Amy thought. She had set them free. She had commuted their sentences.

"What do they want?" Basil asked.

Before she could answer, the penitents were on them, crashing over them like a tide, sending Basil and Amy tossing and turning, submerged in their filthy stench, completely at the mercy of the forces that bore them away. Amy's screams were cut off as she drowned in their attack. The penitents didn't want anything; they were simply bound to the same cycle that had governed their spirits for more than a century. This was who they were. This was what they did.

Basil tried to reach her but was caught up in the mass and swept away. The beam of his flashlight jogged and flashed across the ceiling as he was buried beneath the onslaught.

It was the chair again. They were taking her to the chair. Amy struggled, but their hands were iron bands, caked with ice and freezing mud, lifting her from the floor, raising her kicking and thrashing over their heads. She saw the ceiling spiraling above as she was borne across the floor, catching glimpses in the fragmented light from the flashlight. She could feel herself suddenly dropped, lowered toward a dimly glimpsed wardrobe lying open on the floor like a coffin.

"I'm not going to fit," Amy's mind gibbered to itself as she was pressed into the tight opening. "I'm not going to fit. I'm not going to fit . . . "

The penitents closed the door over her. Bracing her arms, Amy tried to get leverage and push against the lowering wood, but she was fighting gravity. There were too many of them, they were too heavy, and they were pushing down too hard. She managed to stiff-arm the door, holding it up as if bench-pressing it, but she started to feel her elbows bending in the wrong direction, ready to snap. The penitents showed no sign of relenting, so she relaxed her arms and the lid slammed down, a concussive blast of air striking her across the face.

Amy heard something slamming into the surface over and over: *BLAM! BLAM! BLAM! BLAM!* In the tight space, each blow was like a gunshot at point-blank range. It was the sound of nails being driven into her coffin, sealing it shut. Hammering filled the Showroom floor, and the Beehive was alive with the sound of toil once more.

16

INGALUTT

Submit to the panic, fear, and helplessness of drowning, with the hope of death a distant dream. This elegantly designed **INGALUTT** hydrotherapy bath allows the user to suffer this stress again and again until the cure is complete.

AVAILABLE IN NIGHT BIRCH, NATURAL MAPLE, AND GRAY OAK
W 22¾ X D 21¼ X H 68¼
ITEM NUMBER 0056660043

Finally the hammering stopped, leaving only a great silence. Amy was completely immobilized in a wooden box roughly six feet long, twenty inches wide, so shallow that her face touched the lid. It had the dimensions of a coffin, but she knew right away that it was a Liripip, one of the most popular sellers in Wardrobes.

Amy couldn't bend her knees and her right arm was pinned underneath her body. She pressed her left hand against the lid of the wardrobe, but with no leverage it was like trying to move a mountain. Her breath rasped loudly in the tight space. She tried to think rationally. She told herself she couldn't possibly run out of air. There was no way a major corporation like Orsk would make a wardrobe that was airtight. What if a child crawled inside?

But what if this particular Liripip was built airtight by accident? What if the penitents had encased it in sheets of plastic shipping wrap? What if they planned to bury her somewhere in the Beehive? Or what if they hoisted her to some distant shelf in the massive Self-Service Warehouse and left her there? Would anyone be able to hear her? She could be trapped up there for months before someone found her.

Amy screamed. She thrashed and struggled, bruising her shoulders against the sides of the box, but it was no use. She could barely move. And the less she could move, the more she needed to move, the more she needed to *get out right now.*

That's when she felt the water.

At first she thought it was sweat—but it was too cold and there was too much of it. A chilly hand wrapped itself around her right thigh. It was so frigid her feet began to shake inside her Chuck Taylors, and if there had been any light she would've been able to see her own breath.

Amy listened, trying to figure out what was happening, but the raspy sound of her own breathing was too loud. She forced herself to slow her panting until she heard the rustle of her clothes, the high-pitched ringing in her ears. And then, beneath it all, the quiet, steady, implacable sound of water flooding the Showroom and flowing around the Liripip.

Amy rubbed the fingers of her right hand against the back of the wardrobe. They came away wet. Now she could feel the water soaking through her upper sleeve. She rubbed her fingers against the bottom again, and this time she felt standing water; she could actually splash it.

The freezing water continued streaming in, lowering Amy's body temperature, making her teeth chatter. The wardrobe was a stone in the middle of a stream with water rushing past on either side. It suddenly slid to the left. At first Amy thought she was being lifted by the penitents, but as the wardrobe swayed and bobbed she realized she was floating. The flood was lifting her up and carrying her away.

Soon the fingers of her right hand were completely submerged. She realized that in order to breathe she'd have to press her nose against the top of the wardrobe. She screamed and thrashed as the water rose higher and higher, over her arms and knees, filling the Liripip's lower half. In spite of everything that had happened—escaping her chair and escaping the store and rescuing Basil and nearly escaping again—Amy realized she was going to die after all. She was going to drown while trapped inside a Liripip.

And that's when she realized: *you are trapped inside a Liripip.*

The one thing every store partner knew about Liripips was that customers hated them. They were bargain priced so the store sold them in droves, but everyone who purchased one lived to regret it, and irate customers were always carting them back to Returns. Assembling the wardrobe was an exercise in frustration. Four hex screws connected the top to the sides, and fully securing them was almost impossible; even when you did, they fell out at the slightest movement. Liripips on the Showroom floor required constant tightening, which could be done only with Orsk's proprietary Magic Tool. And like all good Orsk employees, Amy carried her Magic Tool at all times.

All she had to do was get it out, reach up inside her coffin, loosen two of the hex bolts at the top, and then pop the lid. With luck the whole frame would come apart, like a badly constructed piece of flat-pack furniture. Under normal circumstances, it would be easy . . . but with an increasingly numbed arm? Submerged in frigid water, trapped in the dark? Water lapped at Amy's ribs and she realized it was her only option.

The first thing to do was to reach into her right pocket. She couldn't do it with her right hand because it was pinned beneath her. She tried to lower her left arm from where it was wedged between her chest and the Liripip's door. Flexing her elbow pushed her hand backward against the door so hard that for a moment she thought she was going to snap her wrist. But she got it past the crisis point and reached down to her waist.

Her fingers clutched at wet folds of empty cloth before rooting deep into something that felt promisingly like a pocket. The muscles in her forearm corded and strained, and suddenly Amy feared the worst. What if she'd lost it? What if it'd fallen out of her pocket when she was running? She tried to look down, but in doing so she banged her forehead so hard against the door that she bit the end of her tongue. Her fingers burrowed, and then she brushed something hard and sharp and tilted her hips, coaxing the item out of her pocket. She snagged the wet metal handle between her fingertips and dragged out the Magic Tool. Now came the hard part.

Somehow Amy had to twist her arm off her chest and raise it above her head. With her left arm resting across her stomach, she began slithering it like a snake toward her face until the pain became too intense—but she forced herself to continue. She whimpered as she pushed her arm farther and farther. With one last superhuman push and a loud gasp, she forced it all the way up, smashing her fingers against the top of the wardrobe, bruising her knuckles and dropping the tool.

Amy resisted panicking until she reached into the water and couldn't find the Magic Tool. The sound from outside was quieter now, but she could feel the wardrobe buffeted by the flow as it filled her coffin, rising inexorably toward the lid. The water was up to her chin now, and her whole body was prickling with cold. It reeked of dirty oil and mud. She felt for the tool underwater, careful not to knock it farther away, but it wasn't there.

It. Wasn't. There.

Had it slipped out a seam? Or had the water pushed it underneath her body, between her shoulder blades, maddeningly out of reach no matter how hard she tried? Amy was all too aware that if the tool had fallen lower than her neck, it was as good as lost. Her elbows weren't double jointed. She would drown.

Forcing her thoughts to slow down, she did what she always did when something was lost: she looked where she least expected to find it. Starting as far away as she could, improbably far from where she'd lost her grip, she felt along the back of the wardrobe, reaching over her head and backward under the water. Her hand was so numb she wasn't sure she'd feel the tool even if she came across it.

Feeling along the bottom, she proceeded in slow sweeps. Then in the most unlikely place, about two inches from the top of her right shoulder, her fingers knocked against something that slid away.

"Gotcha," she whispered.

She stretched more carefully now, and her hand came down right on top of it. Using a fingernail, she pried it off the back of the wardrobe and took a moment to hold it in her palm as tightly as she could.

Clutching the tool, she felt for the top right hex hole. Because her fingers were so numb, it took several tries before she found it. She fed the tool inside and started to turn. For a moment she thought she wouldn't have the leverage to crank the wrench—but then she stretched her arm, mashing her biceps against her nose, and with a sharp crack the bolt began to move.

Amy could rotate it only in a tight semicircle before she had to pull the tool out, turn it back, reseat it, and start again. Every time she went through this ritual, she banged her nose and cheekbones, but she scarcely noticed the pain. Eventually the hex screw came loose and Amy was able to pull it out with her fingers. The right side of her head was now totally underwater, and she heard a satisfying *tak* as the screw touched down on the bottom of the wardrobe. She reached across, found the opposite screw hole, and began the long laborious process of loosening it.

With every crank, her elbow banged the lid of the coffin. But the pain kept her going and soon she found her rhythm: screw, bang, screw, bang, screw, bang, screw, bang. It was taking longer than the first one. Was she doing something wrong? Had she stripped the threads and was now uselessly turning it in the wood? Then suddenly it was out.

Bracing the soles of her shoes against the bottom of the wardrobe, Amy placed her left hand against the top and pushed. For a moment it didn't move, but then the water-softened fiberboard yielded with a crack, the screws on the other side let go of the saturated wood, and the entire top hinged open like a trap door and swirled away. As water flooded into the wardrobe, Amy gripped the sharp lip with both hands and slithered out like a molting snake. She stumbled to her feet. All around her in the darkness she heard the sound of rushing water.

"Basil!" she shouted.

Her eyes instantly located the one source of light on the pitch-black floor. The fallen Maglite was still on, submerged next to an info post and lodged behind a Drazel chest of drawers. Amy sloshed over to it, each step like plunging her legs into a bucket of ice. She stuck her arm into the frigid water up to her elbow and pulled it out.

Immediately she started looking for Basil. Wardrobes had toppled over, and as she watched, the current upended two more and sent them splashing down and tumbling away. Behind her in the distance something was roaring like a waterfall. If she had been nailed inside a wardrobe, it made sense that Basil would be in one, too.

Riding low in the water was a double-doored Finnimbrun wardrobe on its back, encased in a cocoon of clear packing wrap. Amy sloshed over and banged on the door.

"Basil!" she yelled.

She heard a faint cry from inside. She slogged back to the info desk and rummaged in the drawers, yanking them out and letting the contents fall into the water. Normally there were box cutters all over the store, but tonight Amy had to dump out every last drawer before finding a blade at the very bottom. She sloshed back to the wardrobe and slit the plastic with a single swipe. Basil was floating inside. She reached in and hauled him out by his arms, realizing that until that moment she'd been terrified he was dead.

"Ow!" he screamed as she crushed him to her in a sudden hug.

"What's wrong?" she asked, letting go of him.

"They broke my wrist in the door," he said, cradling it.

"They nailed me inside a Liripip," Amy said. "Can you walk?"

"Yeah," he nodded.

She played her flashlight over the Showroom walls, trying to figure out which way to go. Suddenly she froze. "Holy crap."

Torrents gushed from every fake window and every door to nowhere, foaming out in massive sprays, sending furniture tumbling and splashing into the vast oily lake that covered the Showroom floor.

"We need to go," Basil said.

"We have to find Matt and Trinity," Amy said.

"The water's rising too fast," Basil said.

He was right. It was up to their knees now.

"We've got time," Amy said. "This is the second floor. The water won't get any higher."

"Normally, sure," Basil said. "But has a single thing been normal here tonight?"

"So we're just going to leave them?"

"We're lucky we're still alive," Basil stuttered through chattering teeth. "We're minutes away from hypothermia. The water is rising. If we don't leave right now, we might not leave at all."

A Potemkin armchair floated past them, bobbing and bouncing in the current, heading toward the front of the store.

"We have to come back for them," Amy insisted. "Promise me."

"I promise," Basil said, shaking convulsively. "Now, please."

They sloshed toward the front of the store, following the current. In Children's, they waded through a layer of stuffed pandas whose drowned faces grinned at the ceiling. The sound of rushing water was louder up ahead, and the current was picking up speed, threatening to sweep their feet out from under them. When Amy saw what was making the noise, her heart sank. They both stopped, water raging past their legs, and gawked at the stairs that led down to the Market Floor.

Water cascaded in a torrent, foaming into furious rapids. It wasn't just rushing down the stairs, it was pouring from the entire second-floor mezzanine, forming three waterfalls that sent sheer walls plunging down, transforming the stairs into a roaring flume.

"We'll go around," Basil shouted, trying to be heard over the din. "Through the café to the escalator at the front of the showroom. Then down to the main entrance."

Amy swept the flashlight into the café and watched the current snatch three Arsle chairs and suck them down the steps, end over end, where they disappeared in the furious torrent.

"Can you do it?" Amy asked.

Basil nodded, and the two of them walked into the café, away from the raging waterfall on the stairs. The current tore at them. Every time they took a foot off the floor, the water snatched at it, trying to drag them away. Water foamed up to Amy's waist and the greasy spray almost reached her shoulders. She guided Basil in front of her, holding on to his left arm; the right one hung dead at his side. Another Arsle chair tumbleweeded past, sucked toward the stairs; its legs sliced into Basil's shins. He fell, disappearing beneath the waist-deep water.

"Basil!" Amy shouted.

His head surfaced six feet away, moving fast in the direction of the waterfall. Amy ran toward him, trying to keep her footing. Basil couldn't get his legs under him, and he went down again. Amy reached for him, but she wasn't even close. The last thing she saw were his terrified eyes and shouting mouth as he was sucked backward into the foaming rapids of the stairs leading down into the Market Floor.

Amy screamed in frustration. They'd been footsteps away from safety via the escalator. Now she'd have to make her way through the entire Market Floor, then through the Self-Service Warehouse and the checkout lanes before reaching the exit. It was too far, and there was no way of knowing if Basil had even survived his fall.

But he had come back for her. She had to go after him.

Amy sat down in the water and let the current grab her. Next thing she knew she was flying down the stairs, head over heels, the water throwing her, smashing her, sledgehammering her body. When she finally reached the base of the stairs, the rapids hit her like a truck, pushing her deep underwater. Everything was a muffled roar. Amy was seized by panic, unable to tell which way was up.

Something sharp gouged her forehead, then buoyancy dragged her to the surface; she bobbed up, blinking into the darkness as greasy garbage water sheeted down her face. The current was carrying her away from the stairs. Incredibly, she'd managed to hang onto the Maglite, and she shined it across the surface. Basil was hanging onto a nearby pallet of bottled water, clinging to it with his good arm.

"Are you okay?" she asked.

He looked like he was going into shock. His face was gray, his eyes were hollow, and he was shaking so hard he could have been having a seizure. Amy clung to the boxes next to him. "We can take the shortcut through Lighting and cut over to the Warehouse," she said. "Then we swim past the registers and we're out."

It was hard to tell if Basil was nodding or shivering. Amy's left arm, resting on top of the boxes, was caught on something sharp. Instinctively, she yanked it back, pulling something heavy, wet, and black toward her face.

"Ah!" she said, jerking her hand off the cases of water.

A fat black rat plopped into the water and swam away frantically. Amy swept her light across the room. Rats were everywhere. Seething on top of every surface, trying to escape the rising water, the shelves thick with a living carpet of their bodies. They were squirming over one another as they scrambled onto boxes and floating debris, scrabbling for purchase.

The water was heaving with them.

"Go!" Amy shouted.

When Basil didn't move, she grabbed his collar and hauled him out into the dark frigid depths.

The Market Floor was the more conventional part of the Orsk experience, where customers pushed shopping carts past shelves stocked with everyday items: plates, posters, picture frames, spatulas, rolls of shelving paper, glasses, plastic salt and pepper shakers, dish towels, napkins, throw pillows. Now all this merchandise was bobbing in a chest-high river. A cold stink rose off the surface and the darkness was alive with squealing vermin. Amy dragged Basil along by his good arm. The current was at their backs, helping them along, but they were constantly tripping over submerged furniture, flat carts, and electrical cords that wrapped around their legs. "Just a little farther," she assured Basil again and again. "Stay with me."

The entire store reminded Amy of the aftermath of a hurricane. Golf pencils, bottled water, store maps unspooled and softened to delicate membranes, flowerpots, mirrors, rats. Everything was floating free. As they approached the massive Self-Service Warehouse, Amy found she didn't need to walk anymore—she could simply push off the floor and let the current carry her along. She wrapped an arm around Basil's chest, holding him tight, and towed him behind her. It was easier this way; floating along with the debris instead of hacking their way through it.

The current sped up as it rounded the corner and carried them into the cavernous warehouse. The Maglite was useless here, where towering shelves stretched nearly fifty feet to the ceiling. All around

Amy heard creaks and cracks as the flooding stressed the building. Far above her in the darkness, the massive metal shelves loaded with flat packs groaned, and splashes echoed as boxes of Brookas and Müskks fell from higher levels.

Something cracked across Amy's shins and she became entangled in a piece of submerged furniture; she lost her grip on Basil and spun off into a support pillar, nearly dropping her flashlight. She scanned it over the swift-moving water and saw Basil's head and shoulders bobbing away from her.

"Grab that rack!" she yelled.

With his good arm, Basil lunged for one of the massive shelves at the end of the aisle. He clung to it and when he looked back at Amy, his eyes went wide. "Swim!" he yelled. "Don't look back!"

Amy did what anyone would do in that situation. She looked back.

A storm surge of rats was bearing down on her. It was a cresting wave of them, pushed by the current, aimed directly at her face. There were thousands of them surging through the water in a massive swell. She imagined them scrabbling at her lips, worming their way inside her mouth, down her shirt, shrieking and tearing at her. She threw herself forward in a blind panic, swimming fast.

Basil kicked alongside her and together they swam like hell. They made it over the checkout counters, where the ceiling dropped to a standard ten feet. Amy's head brushed past a "See You Soon" banner that hung from the rafters. Squealing echoed in the darkness behind them. Her bruised body ached. Her arms were leaden. Her skin burned from the cold, and her lips were chapped from the oily water.

But they were close. She could see the glass doors to the parking lot. They were mostly submerged but the tops were still visible. Orange light poured through from outside, looking like full daylight after the endless night of Orsk. Amy swam to the motion sensor above the door and waved her hand in front of it. Then she slapped and hammered it with her fist to no avail—the power was off and the doors were locked. Water was exiting through a tiny gap between the glass doors, spraying out onto the sidewalk with a mighty hiss.

"Rats," Basil said, teeth chattering. "Coming."

The hopelessness of the situation overwhelmed Amy. They would drown, separated from fresh air by less than an inch of glass. And the rats were right behind them. This was where the current terminated.

In minutes the water around them would be boiling with rodents clambering over her face, weighing her down, pushing her underwater as they tried to keep themselves on the surface, squealing, tearing, biting, clawing, an aquatic tornado of rats, churning the water, and she and Basil would be torn to shreds or drown.

"Fire extinguisher," she said.

"What?" Basil gasped, struggling to stay afloat.

"Where is it? Which side of the door?"

"Left?" Basil said. "Yeah, left. No, right. Right." He shook his head. "Or left."

Amy locked eyes with him. "I can only do this once."

"Left," Basil said. "It's definitely left."

Amy took a breath and dove.

The water was so full of cleaning chemicals that it burned her eyes, but she forced herself to keep them open. She swam down, pulling herself along the side of the panes, fingers hooking onto the metal runners that separated them, pulling herself deeper and deeper. The cloudy water refracted the beam of the Maglite, bending it into crazy angles, but it was enough. She spotted the red blur of the fire extinguisher to the left of the door and pulled it off its brackets. It was reassuringly heavy in her hands. *In case of emergency, break glass.*

Something solid slammed into her back, tangling in her legs. Amy panicked and thrashed about. By the time she realized it was a Poonang, it was too late. She'd lost the extinguisher, which floated down to dong against the floor and settle on its side.

Amy kicked the chair away and dove after it. Her lungs were burning, but there was no time to go up for air. She swam down the final three feet and gripped the extinguisher. Bracing her feet, she rested the butt end against the panes of the door. Exhaling fully to ease the pressure on her bursting lungs, she drew the extinguisher back to her shoulder and rammed it into the glass.

Water resistance stole all the energy from her thrust, reducing it to a lame tap. The bottom of the extinguisher barely bumped the door. She had no leverage. The glass was too thick. The extinguisher was too heavy. It bounced off the glass, and the heart finally went out of her. The glass was an orange blur. Through it she could dimly see movement. Something was strobing blue and red out there. Sirens? Cops?

Blackness crowded the edges of her vision. *So*

close, she thought to herself. She was so close. All her life, she'd been backing off, falling short, dropping out. Her whole life she had quit. She'd really tried this time, but it was too late.

There was no way she could reach the surface, but maybe she had enough time to try again. One final effort and then she could let herself quit for good.

Last chance.

She placed the base of the extinguisher against the glass, pulled it back three inches, and held steady. Putting everything she had behind her shoulder, she screamed inside her mind and thrust the fire extinguisher forward. It shook in her hands when it hit the pane, and the glass tolled like an underwater bell.

But it didn't break.

Amy felt herself let go, the extinguisher drifting away, her mind leaving her body, her lungs filling with filthy water, the lights dimming lower as she floated down into the dark, down toward the chair that had always been waiting for her.

Then there was a sound like a twig snapping, and a glowing silver line crazed across the glass. It was a crack, bright enough for her to see through the murk. As she watched, it grew with a sound like tearing ice. One end headed toward the upper right corner of the pane, expanding and splintering until water pressure took care of the rest.

With one cataclysmic roar, everything happened at once. The glass burst, exploding into the parking lot, releasing an aquatic avalanche that sucked Amy out with it. Her head smashed into the top of the door as she flew past, and she could feel hot blood flowing as she went spinning, spiraling, soaring through, pinwheeling and tumbling in a deluge of garbage, rats, safety glass, dirty water, and soggy receipt tape onto the sidewalk in front of Orsk.

GURNË 17

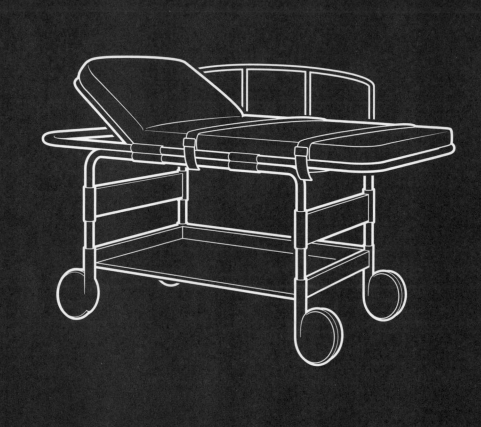

Unwind on the cushion-firm mattress as this elegantly designed wheeled stretcher transfers you to the destination of your choice. Whether it's a fast-paced trip to an urgent care center or a more leisurely cruise to the coroner's office, **GURNË** delivers you in style and comfort.

AVAILABLE IN GALVANIZED STEEL
W 25¾ X L 75¼ X H 31¼
ITEM NUMBER 7743666252

The great gout of water slammed Amy to the sidewalk and then sent her spinning helplessly across the concrete, over the curb, and onto the rough asphalt of the parking lot. Still the water kept coming, pouring out of the store in a massive sideways geyser, a foamy white cataclysm full of squealing rats. One of the creatures smacked into Amy's chest before the current carried it away. She tried to stand in the spray but was instantly knocked back down. Crawling, spitting up water, her knees torn and bloodied, her palms raw hamburger, she managed to drag herself out and collapse on her side. And then she closed her eyes.

"Ma'am, are you all right?"

Twisting her head, Amy looked around for Basil. She spotted him closer to the entrance, surrounded by a trio of firefighters. They were already checking his vitals, asking him questions.

"Ma'am, can you hear me?"

Amy tried to sit up. A very young officer from the

Cuyahoga County sheriff's department was standing over her. He looked all of fourteen years old. She staggered to her feet, his hand on her elbow, then put her arms around the cop and held on to him for dear life while huge wracking sobs tore themselves out of her body.

"I need an EMT," he shouted back over his shoulder. Then, more quietly to Amy, "You've cut your head . . . "

She touched her fingertips to her forehead and felt a bruised flap of skin hanging loose. When she brought her hand away, her fingertips were gray and sticky. The orange parking lot lights leached her blood of color and she stared at it, fascinated. Without a goal, without the urgent need to escape from Orsk, she was in a daze.

A paramedic who looked like a linebacker took her from the cop and guided her to the back of an ambulance. It was bright and white and when he sat her on the rear bumper, she didn't ever want to leave its sane modern light.

"What's your name, miss?" he asked.

"Amy."

He aimed a tiny flashlight at her pupils. "Do you know what day it is, Amy?"

"The day after yesterday."

He smiled. "Can we assume you don't have a horrible brain injury?"

Amy shook her head and tried to smile.

"Don't," the paramedic said. "Try not to move. I'm going to take care of you until we get to the ER."

That sounded good to her. The paramedic popped a thermometer into her ear and checked the reading, then unwrapped a silver space blanket and hung it over her shoulders to stop the shaking. When Amy tried to stand again, he put a hand on her shoulder and coaxed her down. "Just a few minutes," he said. Then he pulled on light-blue latex gloves and went to work on her head.

Cops were stringing yellow tape across the front of the store. Fire trucks were parked at dramatic angles, and firefighters were pressed up to the glass storefront, peering inside. Behind the emergency vehicles, a legion of cars had pulled up and people were everywhere, yelling into their cell phones, holding them up to take pictures, sitting in open driver's-side doors and delivering bad news to someone on the other end of the phone. A gaggle of cops squealed and started dancing a jig as a horde of waterlogged rats ran over their feet.

"There you are! Amy! Thank God you're all right." At the sound of her name, Amy turned dully toward the speaker. Pat, the store's general manager, was jogging over in a Van Halen T-shirt and sweatpants. "Is she okay?" he asked the paramedic.

"So far, so good," the paramedic said, snipping off the last bit of bandage. "A couple of stitches at the ER, keep her warm, she should be fine."

"Thank God," Pat said, turning to Amy. "You look like you might be in shock. Are you in shock? Are you all right? Is she all right?"

"No," Amy said.

"What happened here?" Pat asked. "This is crazy."

Amy looked at the flooded store, still gushing water across the parking lot. Here and there among the cops and firefighters were men and women in windbreakers and sports coats, shouting to one another and speaking into cell phones. One was awkwardly trying to compose an e-mail on a laptop while balancing it in one hand. Amy knew these people had to be the Orsk Consultant Team. They had arrived right on schedule. Amy looked down at her filthy clothes, her shredded Chuck Taylors, her torn jeans.

"I don't know," she finally said to Pat. "Is Basil okay?"

"His arm is broken and he needs a hospital, but yes, he's going to be all right."

"Have you seen the others?"

"Others?" Pat blinked. "There were others?"

"Matt and Trinity. And Ruth Anne. They were all with us."

"Oh, Jesus," Pat said, and he ran-walked to the Consultant Team and started talking to them, pointing frantically at Orsk, gesturing wildly.

Amy walked over to Basil. The firefighters had him propped up on the back of a ladder truck. His face was waxy. Bruises were starting to appear, pushing their way through the tight shiny flesh of his cheekbones. He smiled at Amy, splitting open a wound on his lip. Fresh blood glinted in the lights.

"Ow," he said. "Your head."

"They didn't make it out," Amy said. "I'd hoped they would find a way, but it's just us."

The smile fell from Basil's face and he stood up, wincing at the pain in his arm.

"Son," a firefighter said, "you need to sit down before you fall down."

Basil ignored him and he and Amy walked away from the truck.

"What's Pat doing?" Basil asked.

"What can he do? They'll find their bodies inside after it drains," Amy said.

All the relief she felt at having escaped turned to ashes in her mouth.

"They might not," Basil said. "We don't know what happened in there."

"I do," Amy said. "There was a prison here, and we built a new prison on its ruins, and all the old prisoners came out to give it a try."

Basil kept staring up at the store and then he nodded.

"Yeah," he said. "That sounds about right."

There was a commotion in the parking lot and Amy and Basil turned. A van from 19 Action News was racing across the asphalt, making a beeline for the store. A couple of cops dashed over to intercept it. The consultants from Orsk Regional were retreating to their rental cars.

"How are they going to explain this?" Amy asked.

"They'll figure out something they can live with," Basil said. "Pat's already mentioned the building contractor twice. There will probably be an epic lawsuit."

"What about you? Are they going to blame you?"

"I blame me," he said. "I brought all of you here to save my stupid job. Maybe not Matt and Trinity, but I was still senior supervisor onsite. I was the one who was responsible. I'm the one who got everyone killed."

"That's not true," Amy said.

"Hey! Guys!" Pat was snapping his fingers at them as he came over, holding out his cell phone. "What is this? Is it one of our people?"

Onscreen was a one-word text message: *help*. Amy recognized the number immediately. "It's Matt!" she said. "Call him back."

Pat dialed the number. It rang three times and went to voicemail.

Amy snatched the phone and thumbed a reply: *where r u?*

The three of them stared at the tiny screen for nearly a minute until the phone buzzed back its reply: *help.*

"He's still alive," Amy said. "Matt's still alive."

Pat grabbed the phone and went running off to share the news.

"What's going to happen to him?" Amy asked Basil.

"I don't know," Basil said. "I guess his battery will run out eventually."

The realization settled over them like a shroud.

The silence was broken by the return of the medic. "Miss, we need to head to the ER now," he said. "If your friends are still in the store, the firefighters will find them."

"No, they won't," Amy said.

She and Basil turned and followed the paramedic back to the ambulance. Pat came scrambling after them as the other members of the Consultant Team watched from a distance.

"Look, guys," he began, "hold up. Can we have a minute?" he said to the paramedic.

The paramedic nodded and stepped back a few feet. Pat turned to Amy and Basil.

"I know you've both had a terrible experience and I want to extend my deepest apologies on behalf of Orsk. I also want to assure you guys that whatever happened in there tonight, no one's looking to assign any blame to employees or management. All our losses are covered, okay? Basil? You understand me?"

"Thank you," Basil said.

"Orsk is a family," Pat said. "We take care of one another. The Consultant Team wants you to know this isn't the end of your journey with Orsk. In fact, it's only the beginning. There are two openings—good openings—at the regional office. It's in Pennsylvania, but they pay for relocation and either one of you would be a great fit. Or both of you."

"We're getting promotions?" Basil asked.

"They're desk jobs, but they're salaried, with full benefits." Pat pressed a business card into Basil's hand. Written on the back was a non-Orsk e-mail address. "This is from Tom Larsen himself. He'll be reaching out personally in the next twenty-four hours."

"I don't understand," Basil said.

"The only thing we ask," Pat said, "is that you don't speak to the media. Not for a while. They won't understand what happened here and it'll only lead to confusion. We're going to do a full investigation. We will speak to the architect and the contractors. When we know what happened, we'll share it with you. And when it's time to talk to the press, Orsk will make sure that you guys have good people by your side, people who understand how the media works and how to position your statements. We're going to do right by the two of you, and by Ruth Anne's family."

"And Matt and Trinity," Amy said.

"Well, that's something different," Pat said. "I know you guys say they were here, but I'm sure tonight has been very confusing, and it was probably hard to know exactly what was going on. They weren't on the clock, you know."

"They were here," Amy said.

"I know you *believe* that," Pat said. "But this situation is challenging enough without adding more people to the mix. Let's not start making up things that sound worse."

"They were here," Amy repeated. "I saw them. I dragged Trinity halfway through the store. I spoke to Matt. I'm not crazy."

"No one's saying you are," Pat said. "But what we're wondering is that if they weren't on the clock, and if Basil wasn't paying them, are they really our responsibility? Here you go, Amy."

He held out a second business card. It bore the same address handwritten on the back. Amy felt something building inside her chest, and when she spoke her voice was cold.

"So we just keep quiet and we keep our jobs?" she asked.

"Better jobs," Pat said. "It's a win-win."

"Are you serious? Three of your employees are dead, and you're trying to bribe us?" Amy knocked the business card away. "You can keep your better jobs, Pat. We'd rather pick up cans by the side of the road than work another day for Orsk. Right, Basil?"

"I know you're upset—" Pat began.

"Upset?" Amy's voice was loud. The anchorwoman with the news crew heard her, grabbed her cameraman, and tried to jockey around the line of cops to get closer. The Orsk consultants looked alarmed. "People died, I almost died, and the first thing you want to do is control your liability? Do you know how messed up that is?"

"Amy, stop it," Basil said. "He's right. What's done

is done. They weren't supposed to be here."

Amy felt like she'd been slapped.

"You're going along with this?" she asked.

"I want to get all outraged too," Basil said. "But this isn't our responsibility anymore. Leave it to the professionals. They'll do the right thing. I've got my little sister to take care of. Just be happy they're giving us something."

A monstrous bird unfurled its wings inside Amy's chest and her anger felt bigger than the world. Everything they had done, all the horrors inside the store, it was as if none of it had happened. She felt lonelier than ever before in her life.

"I'm truly sorry about what happened," Pat said. "We will privately extend our condolences to the families. We will talk to the architects and the contractors and we will hold them accountable for this tragedy. We will work something out so that everyone's protected. You and Basil cannot blame yourselves for this turn of events. Matt and Trinity and Ruth Anne were not your responsibility."

Amy swung at his head. She'd never hit another person before, and the result was something between a slap and a punch, surprising Pat more than hurting him.

"You asshole," she shouted. "That's exactly what they were!"

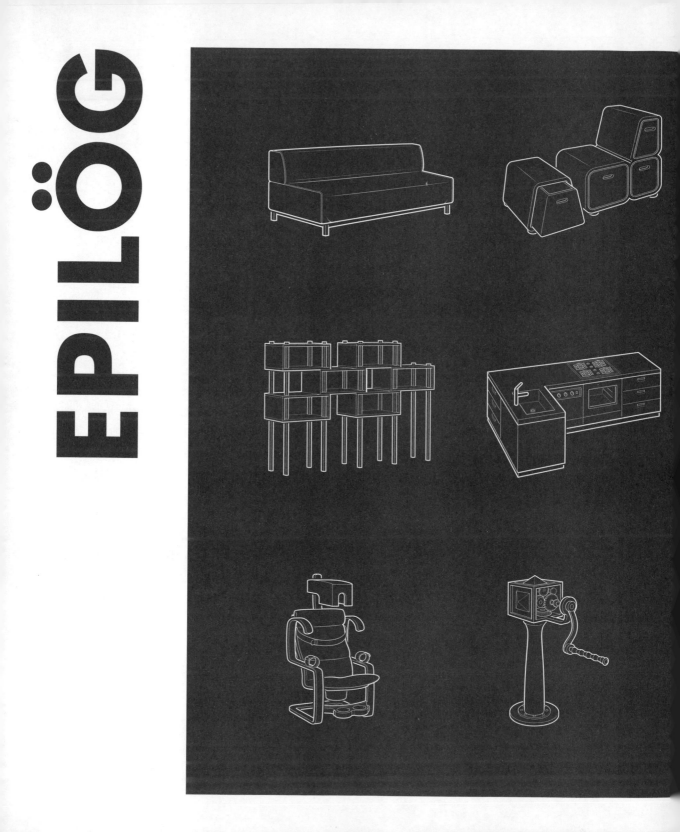

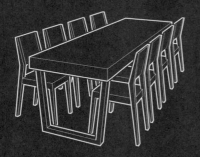

Orsk did come up with an answer it could live with: a massive water main break, coupled with a complete malfunction of the sprinkler system. When insurance adjusters finally got into the store, they found the false doors sealed, the wardrobes shattered, no penitents, no bodies, and no proof of anything beyond an enormous flood. The entire inventory was written off as a loss.

Matt, Trinity, and Ruth Anne were never found. Orsk paid for their memorial services and provided a settlement to the families. In the case of Matt and Trinity, they handled things quietly, without any admission that the two of them had been in the store. There was additional arbitration between the corporate offices, the building contractors, and the architectural firm, but no one sued and no one spoke to the press. As for Carl, his body was never found and his name never appeared in any of the articles about the disaster. Amy didn't know if that was because he was homeless or because he had never existed, but she seemed to be the only person on earth who remembered him.

There were three memorial services: one for Matt, one for Trinity, and one for Ruth Anne. Trinity's was closed to anyone who wasn't a member of her church. Matt's was packed with his friends from high school and community college, and there were several meaningful readings and a really bad singer with too much vibrato. Basil was there, but Amy avoided him. One hundred thirty-four people went to Ruth Anne's memorial. Every single one of them was an Orsk employee or customer. They gave eulogies, cried, talked about the little kindnesses she had shown them. Snoopy was sitting on a table at the front surrounded by flowers and framed photos. A lot of people wore their Orsk uniforms. Amy stood in the back for half of the service and then she left, feeling more numb than when she'd arrived.

A week after the events at the store, the Orsk legal department contacted Amy, writing that the company considered all of its partners to be part of the Orsk family and claiming that it wanted to demonstrate its goodwill. If Amy would sign a release and covenant not to sue, Orsk would, without admitting any responsibility or wrongdoing, write her a check for a generous severance. Amy didn't care. She signed the paper without even reading it. The check arrived via DHL ninety days later. It was for $8,397.

She couldn't sleep. That first night, her mom's new husband, Gerard, picked her up at the ER and brought her home to the trailer. Her mom had been too upset to think straight, so she'd taken a pill and gone to bed before they arrived. Amy turned on every single light and closed all the curtains. She told Gerard an edited version of what had happened, a version without the penitents, or the tunnels, or being nailed in wardrobes, but even then it still sounded unreal, and she could tell he thought she was lying. After a while, he went to bed and she was left alone. Exhausted but still too scared to be on her own, she dragged a pillow and blanket into her mom's bedroom and lay on the floor at the foot of the bed, unable to close her eyes.

The next day, Amy kept dozing off at random moments: in the middle of lunch, while trying to talk to her mom, while talking to her old roommates on the phone. They called her four times before she answered and put her on three-way calling to tell her how brave she was, and what a hero she was for surviving, and asking her what it was really like. After a few minutes, they realized she wasn't going to give them the juicy answers they wanted, and then it was just a matter of figuring out how to end the call in the least awkward way possible.

A few days later, Gerard drove to her apartment and picked up her stuff. Amy never knew it, but he wound up writing a check to cover the rent she owed. He helped Amy move her boxes back into her old bedroom, but she never unpacked. She wore the same sweatpants every day and spent most of her time sleeping.

Her mom made a fuss at first and even Gerard seemed to be having an Amy renaissance, but eventually their general disappointment crept back in. It didn't take long. Gerard delicately raised the subject of her going back to community college or getting another job. Any job. It didn't have to be retail. She could be a dog walker. She just needed to do something. She couldn't sit in her bedroom watching TV for the rest of her life.

But that was exactly what Amy wanted to do. She watched a lot of *Real Housewives of Wherever* until she realized that she had seen every episode of every season at least twice. Then she started buying movies on iTunes, racking up $147 in charges in one week. Basil e-mailed her five times, but she deleted his messages without reading them. Reading took too much concentration. She tried a few grief and trauma books, she even picked up the Bible and ordered a Koran from Amazon, but after reading a couple of sentences her mind would wander and eventually she'd give up.

For the first week after the disaster, she followed the news religiously, watching everything about Orsk with a feverish intensity. But after a few days the story slipped from the headlines, and so did her interest. She ate, she slept during the day, she ignored questions from her mom and Gerard until they stopped asking them. She existed.

Six months passed. Seven months. Amy stayed in her room over Christmas, and her mom drove out to see her aunts and uncles without her. She fell asleep at 6 p.m. on New Year's Eve and woke up at three in the morning and couldn't fall back to sleep for two days. January came and went. February passed. Each day was crossed off on the calendar, and each day was just like the one before.

Sometimes Amy cried for no reason. She'd spend hours experiencing either great wracking sobs or tears silently streaming down her face that she couldn't explain. March passed. April. Gerard and her mom went on vacation to see her cousins in Niagara Falls without her. Staying in the trailer alone was too much, so she checked into a hotel while they were gone. Otherwise, Amy didn't go outside, she didn't talk, she refused therapy. She just slept when she could, and ate, and existed.

And then, one day, she discovered what she had to do.

After the flood, after the newspaper stories, after a segment on *Hardball with Chris Matthews* in which a spokesperson for Orsk USA fielded questions about his company's commitment to the safety of its employees, after the memorial services, Orsk slipped out of town. The building was infested with toxic black mold. It needed to be torn down and rebuilt, and Tom Larsen had no interest in making a huge investment in a store with so many negative associations. It was better just to cut and run.

To everyone's surprise, another big box retail store bought the property. Thirteen months after the disaster, Planet Baby opened in the same location. A one-stop retail shopping solution for all your baby's needs. With Planet Baby, having a baby wasn't just the greatest choice you could ever make—it was the start of a thrilling new lifestyle.

The day she read about the opening, Amy drove out and completed a job application. She couldn't believe it when the next day someone in HR called her cell phone, explaining she'd been hired as an assistant floor manager. She hid the news from Gerard and her mom for as long as possible. The night before she started the job, she revealed her plan. Their happiness was qualified, but Gerard seemed to speak for both of them when he said: "We're glad you're getting back on the horse that threw you, because we think it's time you started contributing to the rent. That settlement isn't going to last forever."

The morning of her first shift, Amy dosed herself with Visine, drank six cups of coffee, started up her old Honda Civic, and drove the route she remembered so well, taking the feeder road to River Park Drive. Out of habit, she pulled into the parking space she'd always used, around the side of the building, back when it was Orsk, before it was Planet Baby.

The store was different but the same. The muted color scheme had been replaced with bright primary hues. Signs that looked like an unusually literate toddler had scrawled them in crayon hung everywhere, reminding Mommy and Daddy to buy all the right things for Baby who needed them so badly but could not yet communicate his (or her) wishes, so Planet Baby was generously interpreting them for him (or her). Thank you, Planet Baby.

Inside, Amy reported to the back of house and met the head of HR. She had bought her own uniform and went to the locker room to change into the soft denim jeans and smocklike pink shirt that erased her shape. No one here wore Chuck Taylors. She noticed it was all Reeboks, pink for girls, blue for boys. Amy made a note to buy a pair. She wanted to fit in.

She was running a few minutes late, so her shift sponsor guided her across the massive floor to an orientation tour that was already in progress. There were some of the same room displays as in Orsk, placed in some of the same areas, with a significant emphasis on playrooms, nurseries, and baby's first big boy (or big girl) bedroom. Amy was quietly pleased to note that several of the rooms had fake doors nailed to the walls, to complete the illusion that customers were peering inside an actual house.

The sponsor took her through Planet Baby's winding aisles and crammed displays, chattering all the while, until they finally reached a group of trainees listening to the floor manager. "We want to guide customers but not overwhelm them," he was saying. "Planet Baby is a total experience, but it should always be a good experience. First retail contact is vital."

The manager giving the orientation nodded to acknowledge Amy's arrival and then returned to his speech.

"There are two kinds of shopper at Planet Baby," he continued. "Those who buy nothing, and those who buy everything. Up here in the Showroom, it's less about acquisition and more about aspiration. The serious shopping doesn't happen until they get downstairs into what we like to call the Baby Store."

Amy settled back and let the familiar retail hypnosis wash over her again. Her shift ended at six o'clock and she enjoyed a leisurely meal at Panera Bread, just up Route 77. Then she stopped at Dick's Sporting Goods and Home Depot for a couple of last-minute purchases. Then she returned to the Planet Baby parking lot and waited.

The cleaning team arrived at eleven o'clock—a stream of yellow-shirted custodians swiping their way through the partners' entrance. Amy opened her car door and tightened the straps on her backpack. It was heavy but only because it was full of flashlights, batteries, a screwdriver, a knife, five hundred yards of fishing line, a hundred-foot roll of glow-in-the-dark tape, motion sickness patches, and three of Planet Baby's own Magic Tools. She wasn't getting lost in the tunnels this time. She would use the tape and fishing line to mark her path, and when she found the others she would lead them back out again.

The last of the custodians was a short stocky guy with a goatee and neck tattoos. As he passed his card over the reader and entered the building, Amy sprinted toward the entrance, flying over the asphalt, trying to catch the door before it closed. She wasn't going to make it. She'd parked too far away. She reached for the knob, but her fingertips barely grazed it and the door slammed shut. She kicked the base of it, hard.

"Let me get that," a voice said.

She turned and saw Basil walking up. He'd gained a couple of pounds, but his face had healed nicely. There was the small worm of a scar bulging from his chin, a slight twist of a scar in his left eyebrow. He wore a repetitive stress injury brace on his right forearm. He had his Planet Baby ID card out.

"I thought I saw your name on the schedule," he said. "What's in the backpack?"

There was no way in hell she was telling this backstabber anything. But she couldn't resist a dig.

"Too bad your big career with Orsk Corporate didn't work out," she said. "It must have taken some serious surgery to extract you from all the way up Tom Larsen's ass."

"I never e-mailed him," Basil said. "I couldn't do it. I wound up working in a McDonald's for most of last year."

"Well, goodie for you," Amy said. "You grew some morals."

"I've been here three months," Basil said. "Deputy operations manager. What's in the backpack?"

"I have to go," Amy said, turning away. "If you see me on the floor, don't talk to me. We have nothing to do with each other, you understand?"

"I bet it's the same stuff I've got in mine," Basil said. "Flashlights, batteries, pocket hand warmers, I even brought some pepper spray, although I'm not sure if that'll work on those things. I was just on my way to pick it up."

Amy's fury drained away, replaced by confusion.

"What are you talking about?" she asked.

"They were my friends, too," he said. "More important, they were my responsibility. I tried telling you that before, but you weren't listening." He lowered his voice to a whisper. "I already stayed once, by the way. The doors are still open. The Beehive's still there."

"How about Matt? Or Trinity? Did you see them?"

"Not yet," Basil said. "Is that why you're here?"

"I'm getting them out," she said, nodding. "Everyone keeps telling me it's all over, that it's back to normal, but I don't want to go back to normal. I don't like the person I used to be. I want to keep being the person I was that night."

"It might be harder than you remember," Basil said. "The penitents are less organized without their leader. Easier to evade. But the store still gets inside your head, and all the baby merch makes it extra freaky. You want to avoid looking inside the cribs, understand?"

"I'm going to go slow and careful," Amy said. "I'm going to figure out how this place works, and I'm going to keep coming back again and again until I find them. Day and night, I'm not quitting until it's over."

They almost smiled at each other before Amy looked away. The air was humid and the frogs were roaring in the marsh. She heard an electronic *eep* as Basil swiped his ID over the scanner. The lock clicked inside the doorframe, and he held the door wide.

Bugs flew in, attracted by the light. Amy wanted to say something, to reassure him that she'd changed, to tell him she was glad he'd come back, she was glad she'd been wrong about him. Instead, she just stepped inside the door. There was no more time to waste. They had work to do.

ORSK: THE BETTER HOME FOR THE EVERYONE!

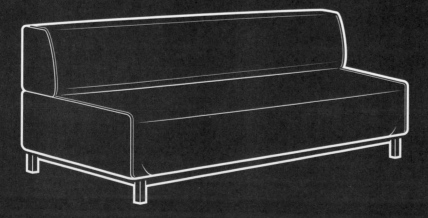

ORSK

Orsk USA would like to acknowledge the following partners for their support:

Thanks to Alexandre Saldaña and Claudia Hipolito of Orsk, Fargo, for assisting local authorities during their store's recent HR crisis.

Welcome to Stine Moen, our new liaison with law enforcement in the European Union, and John Joseph Adams, new store manager at Orsk, Innsmouth.

Farewell to Matt London of Orsk, Round Rock. Jordan Hamessley will be taking over his duties and we are grateful for her leadership.

Thanks to regional managers Katarina Gligorijevic and Colin Geddes for leading renewed staffing efforts across Orsk Canada.

Finally, Orsk USA continues to extend our deepest sympathies to the family and friends of Amanda Cohen, who remains missing three months after an overnight team-building exercise at Orsk, North York. Any information regarding her whereabouts should be directed to local authorities.

We never stop.
We never sleep.
And now we're in your home.

ORSKUSA.COM

Wherever you go, Orsk will be there. Always. That's the Orsk Guarantee. Our website and mobile app provide a one-on-one experience that allows Orsk to follow you everywhere. Spend hours or days immersing yourself in our vast digital presence. It's like entering another world!

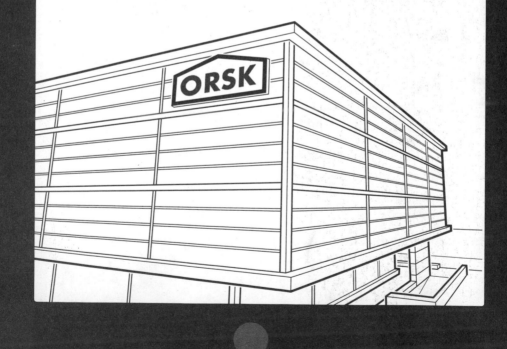